THE SEVEN SIGNS

③

For Ava and Clare

Scholastic Australia
345 Pacific Highway Lindfield NSW 2070
An imprint of Scholastic Australia Pty Limited
PO Box 579 Gosford NSW 2250
ABN 11 000 614 577
www.scholastic.com.au

Part of the Scholastic Group
Sydney • Auckland • New York • Toronto • London • Mexico City •
New Delhi • Hong Kong • Buenos Aires • Puerto Rico

Published by Scholastic Australia in 2017.
Text copyright © Michael Adams, 2017.
Cover design by Blacksheep Design Ltd UK.
Cover copyright © Scholastic Australia, 2017.
Cover images: small silhouette figures © Zurijeta/Shutterstock.com; small silhouette figure ©
Jacek Chabraszewski/Shutterstock.com.

Internal illustrations by Blacksheep Design Ltd UK.
Internal images: infinity © Absemetov/Shutterstock.com; supersonic aircraft © Rikko/
Shutterstock.com; speed lines background © YoPixArt/Shutterstock.com.

National Library of Australia Cataloguing-in-Publication entry:
Creator: Adams, Michael Edwin, 1970- author.
Title: Wipeout / Michael Adams.
ISBN: 9781743628034 (paperback)
Series: Adams, Michael Edwin, 1970- Seven signs; 3.
Target Audience: For children.
Subjects: Adventure stories.
        Cyberterrorism--Juvenile fiction.
Dewey Number: A823.4

Typeset in Archer and Gotham.

Printed in Australia by McPherson's Printing Group, Maryborough, Victoria.

Scholastic Australia's policy, in association with McPherson's Printing Group, is to use papers
that are renewable and made efficiently from wood grown in responsibly managed forests,
so as to minimise its environmental footprint.

10 9 8 7 6 5 4 3 2 1   17 18 19 20 21 / 1

THE SEVEN SIGNS

3

WIPEOUT

MICHAEL ADAMS

A Scholastic Australia Book

Yasmin was rescued after the Cairo–Alexandria train crash and taken to Alexandria, where she and Zander are meeting with Professor Samir Abbass, a symbology expert, at the Library of Alexandria.

Andy and Dylan are wanted suspects in the murder of the actor, Ryder White, who hoaxed them into making a false *Scoop* video. The video discredited both Andy's journalistic credibility as well as tarnishing Felix Scott's reputation.

Isabel, Mila and JJ broke down the clues in the Second Sign, mistakenly thinking that Colombia was the target.

As the countdown ended, Yasmin and Zander discovered that the Second Sign predicted all the AutoDrive cars would go haywire in LA, the car capital of the world.

After a deadly series of car crashes, and facing further disaster with colossal fires from exploding oil wells, Andy and Dylan may never make it to the SpaceSkimmer for the next leg of their DARE winner adventure ...

In Egypt, the other DARE winners begin to realise how dangerously deep The Signmaker's obsession runs.

If you could be a hero, would you DARE?

Everything around them seemed to be on fire—the sky, the ground, the road and traffic. Blown through the air by the landscape exploding behind them, Andy and Dylan tumbled in a world of flame and roaring noise, smoke and intense heat. They hit the road. Smacked hard onto the bitumen. Rolled and scraped and bumped to a stop against the steel crash barrier on the side of the highway.

Crumpled, gasping and scorched, they looked at each other frantically and then up at the orange flames swirling across low smoke clouds. The fire wanted them. Sought to burn them to ash and bone. No time for a last breath, let alone last words.

But then . . . the tsunami of flames rolled away.

Like water rushing back out to sea, Andy thought desperately, *another wave might be coming!*

'Quick, cover!' Barely able to hear himself over the ringing in his ears, Andy scrambled beside a wrecked Chevy. Dylan dived down beside him as another ball of fire ripped into the sky over what had been a luxury golf course. The blast wave blew out windshields and set more car alarms whooping. Pressed shoulder to shoulder, Andy and Dylan shook as the road shuddered beneath them. They huddled until the heat and howling eased.

Risking a look up through the car's jagged windows,

the boys saw the golf course's greens and sand traps had become fiery lakes and smoking craters. Like a vision from the dawn of time—or from the end of the world. On the road, people ran between ruined vehicles, desperate to find shelter. Back over the wetlands, where their AutoTaxi had crashed, police helicopters winched survivors to safety.

The boys ducked back down.

'Mate, are you all right?' Dylan shouted, brushing cubes of window glass from his singed dreadlocks.

Andy's face was sooty and his blond hair was filthy with mud. His blue eyes were red-rimmed—from tears, from nearly drowning, from stinging smoke. Despite it all, he nodded. 'I think so,' he said loudly. 'You?'

Dylan's dark skin was streaked with ash. His knee bled through his torn slacks and his chest was grazed through his ripped Hawaiian shirt. 'I'll live,' he said, adjusting the glasses he'd managed to keep intact through all of it. 'What the hell happened?'

'Oil pipeline,' Andy blurted. 'They're everywhere under the city. One must've blown.'

Dylan sniffed. 'Is that what I can smell?'

Andy stiffened as the sharp fumes hit his nostrils. 'That's not oil!'

In terror, the boys looked down and around. They were crouching in a rainbow-glinting puddle—petrol! It was leaking from the Chevy's ruptured fuel tank. One spark and they'd be cremated!

Another boom shook the world. Fire shot into the air over

the golf course, spraying burning clumps of turf high into the sky, sending rescue choppers scattering in all directions.

'Go!' shouted Dylan.

The boys bolted up and away from the car.

Skin stinging from his fuel-soaked clothes, Dylan hoped they weren't dripping a petrol trail any fire could follow. A terrified glance back told him they were about to find out. A burning clump of turf streaked from the sky and hurtled like a meteor towards the Chevy. 'Down!' he yelled.

Andy and Dylan threw themselves behind a bus stop as the blazing ball slammed into the car's roof and—

Whoosh-kabooooom!

—turned the pool of petrol into a fireball.

The vehicle detonated, sending a heat wave scorching down the road. Then the car beside it blew—and the next car, then another—closer and closer to where the boys sheltered.

Boom! Boom! Boom!

'Chain reaction!' Andy screamed. 'Run!'

Arms and legs hammering, they dodged between cars, trying desperately to keep ahead of the blasts. But the heat grew more intense, and deadly debris sizzled through the air all around them.

'Down here!' Andy screamed, leaping over a safety rail.

Dylan jumped after him, the earth falling away for a moment before the ground rushed up and he tumbled down an embankment into a weedy vacant lot.

'Uuuumpfh!' he groaned, coming to rest beside Andy in a ditch.

The boys hugged the ground as cars exploded on the highway above them. Hot metal and broken glass rained down, clinking and tinkling where it hit the dirt. When the rumbling stopped, they dared to stick their heads up. The road up there was an inferno. Streams of burning petrol sloshed down the embankment. They would be engulfed in seconds.

Dylan jumped up, pointing desperately across the vacant lot stretching away from them. They had to get away. Andy sprang to his feet and raced with Dylan across the rocky ground. Looking back, they saw the fuel had turned the ditch into a blazing river. But at least the fire was contained. When they got to the other side of the lot they could take side streets to the airport.

'Almost there,' Andy panted as they reached the tall chain-link fence on the far side.

Dylan nodded, and tried to summon the strength to climb. He cocked his head, struggling to make out a noise over his ringing ears and the roaring world.

Andy's frown said he heard it, too.

Rising above the rumbling. Horrible protesting bellows. Louder and louder. Not human. Metal on metal. A machine in its death throes.

Fff-fff-ffarrscree-creech!

The boys whirled just as a burning police chopper spun out of the smoke clouds and spiralled straight at them.

'The official death toll now stands at sixty-eight, but it is likely to climb rapidly,' said a TV news anchor, struggling to keep her composure as a video window showed the road carnage that had ripped through California. 'From what we understand so far, a large number of AutoDrive cars on the state's roads veered out of control. Hundreds, or even thousands, of crashes have sparked fires and chaos. Adding to the emergency, the inferno has ignited an oil pipeline, which is now blazing uncontrollably near Los Angeles airport.'

Shocked and worried faces filled the HoloSpace in Professor Samir Abbass's office in the Library of Alexandria. Isabel, Mila and JJ had called as soon as they received Yasmin's text telling them the symbols pointed to California. Now they all watched in horror as the HoloSpace showed choppers hovering over wetlands filled with crashed cars. Where were Andy and Dylan?

'This is . . .' the professor started to say. The big man with the afro tugged at his bow tie, lost for words at what he'd seen and heard in the short time since meeting Yasmin and Zander. 'It's . . . it's . . .'

'Unbelievable,' Zander finished.

In the chair beside him, Yasmin nodded, almond eyes shimmering, freckled cheeks glistening with tears.

'How could I have been so wrong about the attack being

on Colombia!' Isabel fumed from her end of the HoloSpace as she paced. 'I feel so guilty!'

Mila jumped up to hug her friend. 'No, this is not your fault!'

'We all fell for it,' JJ said from his Seoul bedroom.

'Andy and Dylan,' Yasmin said, 'could they have survived?'

Zander's eyebrows arched. 'Hopefully your warning text reached them in time. If they were off the road, they should be OK.'

Yasmin thought he sounded like he was trying to convince himself.

'Let's try to call Andy and Dylan again,' Mila said.

From the moment they'd heard what happened in California, they had tried repeatedly to contact the boys, but they hadn't answered their phones.

'Request cannot be completed,' a computerised voice said now. 'Please try again later.'

'Miss Chen has to know more than we are getting from the news,' Zander said, slipping on his SmartGlasses. 'I am going to try her.' His eyes flitted behind his lenses for a moment before he shook his head. 'No answer.'

'With everything that's happened, she's probably crazy-busy,' JJ said.

'I do not care,' Zander said, getting to his feet, his darkly handsome features set in determination. 'She's parked right outside. I am going out to the car. She will have to talk to me then. Maybe she can track Andy's and Dylan's phones.'

Yasmin tucked a wisp of brown hair beneath her head-scarf and nodded. 'Yes, go, find out what you can! Hurry!'

'Back soon,' he said. 'Sit tight.'

The DARE winners and the professor watched the news in shocked silence. Aerial footage streaming from a news drone showed a city street filled with smashed cars. Dozens of vehicles bobbed in a river where they had veered off a bridge. Oil derricks burned beside a golf course that looked like a volcanic landscape. Another video showed a passenger in an Infinity AeroCar prototype plucking survivors from a smoky roadside and whisking them to safety.

Off to one side of the news windows, the Games Thinker website counted down again mercilessly.

12:36:22

'When that runs out, there will be new symbols, the Third Sign?' the professor asked quietly.

The DARE winners nodded.

'And when the next countdown runs out,' Isabel said gravely, 'comes the third attack.'

'Not if we can help it,' JJ said. 'Next time we'll . . .'

He couldn't finish his sentence. Bravado sounded hollow. Especially when they'd failed so spectacularly to stop the second attack. The footage from California was terrible evidence of that.

And somewhere among the flames Andy and Dylan were fighting for their lives.

Sitting at the centre of the hi-tech network like a thousand-eyed spider inside a vast web, The Signmaker watched California descend into chaos. An army of hacked phones, dash cams and surveillance systems streamed live images into the HQ's huge HoloSpace. A dozen TV channels provided updates on the death and destruction, already putting the human toll at nearly one hundred and the economic damage in the billions. Satellite images showed damage from all over the state, while news websites urgently beamed the press conferences being given by the governor and the president.

As much as The Signmaker took no pleasure in the pain the plan was causing, all that fire and fear and fury were music to the mastermind's ears. The Signmaker was the composer and conductor of an orchestra that was playing a perfectly executed symphony of destruction. The truly devastating crescendo was still five days away, when the world would learn an unforgettable lesson. After that, everything would be different. From destruction would come creation.

There was no way to know if Andy and Dylan had survived the carnage. They had ducked the Infinity AeroCar that would have ensured their safety. Since then their phones had gone dead and were untrackable. The

Signmaker wanted them alive. The boys—and their DARE friends—had important roles to play. They had to witness everything, had to understand, had to *believe*. They needed to comprehend the world as it was and how The Signmaker would remake it. But all in good time.

For now, the DARE winners were proving worthy adversaries in the game. Their battle to beat the clock and save the world was crucial to the outcome, crucial to the birth of the new world.

But The Signmaker was disturbed they had figured out the Second Sign before the Californian carnage had been unleashed. If they had succeeded in decoding it even an hour earlier, they might have alerted American authorities and ruined everything. The professor was to blame for that. He had been too much help to them. This game was for the DARE winners. Samir Abbass was only ever meant to be a diversion. Now he was a distraction. One that needed to be dealt with.

The Signmaker grinned, fist uncurling to release thousands of microscopic nanobots. The swarm would lie in wait, ready to play their part in the endgame when the time came.

But before that, the Third Sign would be revealed. The stakes would be more deadly and the riddles more devilish.

The Signmaker smiled, thinking of the symbols waiting to be unleashed.

The out-of-control helicopter spun wildly towards the boys. Frenzied rotors chopped the air, fire billowed from its engines and the pilot fought a desperate battle for control. Andy and Dylan had nowhere to run. It was on a crash course for where they stood, frozen, by the fence. Then, suddenly, as if grabbed midair by an invisible hand, the chopper snagged on powerlines that stretched high across the field. It strained for a second, caught, rotors slicing into sparking cables, and then swung down fast and slammed into the middle of the vacant lot.

Kerrbrgggh!

The chopper erupted, coming apart in geysers of fire.

Inside the fire, the chopper's cabin was a black and burning carcass. There was no way to help whoever had been on board. Even so, Andy took a shocked step towards the blazing wreckage. Dylan gently caught his arm.

'Mate, don't,' he whispered. 'There's nothing we can do. Plus, one ember and you're done for, too.'

Andy nodded, looking at his petrol-soaked clothes, and wiped smudged tears from his cheeks. 'I . . . I . . .'

There were no words. But he didn't have to say anything. Dylan knew everything he felt. He was living this nightmare, too.

'We have to go,' the Aussie said. 'Come on, OK?'

Summoning the energy to keep moving, the boys hauled themselves over the chain-link fence and limped along side streets before they joined a stream of panicked survivors on the road to the Los Angeles airport. Desperate to reach the safety of the airport, Andy and Dylan weaved around people nursing minor injuries and skirted small groups huddling on the pavement in shock. When they finally reached LAX's long terminal and could see through the airport's huge glass windows, they saw bigger crowds gathered around news screens showing the Los Angeles carnage.

Andy and Dylan hurriedly zeroed in on the Infinity Air entrance. Inside, a security guard saw them, frowned and then turned and shouted urgently. A scowling woman in a black suit rushed from the crowd. She looked all business—bad business—with a satellite phone in one hand and a nasty-looking machine pistol swinging from a shoulder strap. The boys looked at each other nervously as she barked an order to the guard who then opened the door.

'Andy? Dylan?' she said. 'Matilda Johnson. Infinity Security. Get in here!'

The boys rushed into the Infinity Air terminal and stood bent, hands on hips, heaving for breath as the guard locked the door behind them.

'Are you injured?' Matilda demanded.

Andy and Dylan straightened. While they were muddy, bloody, battered and stank of petrol, they would be fine with a shower, a change of clothes and a few HealFast strips. But the same couldn't be said for untold numbers of others.

'We're fine,' Dylan said. 'We were lucky.'

'Lucky.' Andy nodded but his eyes had a far-off look. Being locked up in custody meant his dad was safe from crazy cars. But what about Andy's school friends? He silently hoped they had been safe in their homes when the morning roads became disaster zones.

'Follow me,' Matilda ordered.

Andy and Dylan trailed her through the Infinity Air lounge, which teemed with panicky passengers.

'Cell and landline networks are in chaos,' Matilda said. 'There's patchy internet but I have satellite comms. Miss Chen called from Egypt. She said that last she'd heard, you were on your way to the airport and your evacuation was a priority.'

The boys raised their eyebrows as Matilda stopped to take a call on her satellite phone.

'Miss Chen's worried about our safety?' Dylan whispered. 'What the hell?'

'If she's The Signmaker,' Andy said in a low voice, 'didn't she just try to *kill* us?'

Dylan frowned. 'Maybe she actually tried to save us.'

'The Infinity AeroCar! We would've been safe in it, wouldn't we?' Andy realised.

Dylan nodded. 'Yeah. I saw Infinity AutoCars pulling over just before everything went crazy.'

'What does it mean?' Andy asked.

Dylan shook his head. 'No idea. Just like I've got no idea what Miss Chen is up to now.'

'Maybe,' Andy mused quietly, 'she's trying to help us to put herself above suspicion.'

'Come on!' Matilda urged, sat-phone holstered, as she led the boys through a security door. At the far end of an empty lounge, uniformed pilots checked computer monitors beside windows overlooking two SpaceSkimmers on the tarmac.

'Situation report?' Matilda demanded.

A red-haired pilot turned. Her name badge identified her as Captain Mia Demelo. 'Word is, the president's going to shut down US airspace,' she said.

Andy and Dylan looked at each other and groaned. Getting out of LA was the only way they could help prevent the next attack and bring down The Signmaker.

'But I'm supposed to evac these guys,' argued Matilda.

'Ma'am,' drawled a pilot as he turned from the computer monitor. The boys saw his face was terribly scarred under his cap.

'I'm listening,' Matilda said.

'We haven't received official word, so as long as we stick to our original flight plans and passenger lists,' continued the pilot whose badge said he was Captain Danny Hunt, 'I think those SpaceSkimmers can still take off for Seoul and Bogotá. So let's shake our tail feathers and get these birds outta here!'

All eyes flew to Zander as he appeared in the doorway.

'Andy and Dylan?' Yasmin blurted. 'Are they OK?'

Zander whipped off his SmartGlasses and broke into a smile. 'Yes! While I was waiting to speak to her, Miss Chen was on the phone to Los Angeles. Andy and Dylan are safe.'

'Oh, what a relief!' Yasmin threw her arms around him.

In the HoloSpace, Mila and Isabel grinned ear to ear while JJ did a little victory hop around his bedroom.

A little embarrassed, Yasmin let go of Zander. 'Where are they?' she asked, stepping back. 'Are they hurt?'

'Apparently, they are fine,' he reassured her. 'Miss Chen said they are about to fly out of Los Angeles.'

'Where to?' Isabel asked.

'Bogotá and Seoul—the original flight plans,' Zander replied. 'I guess you will be seeing Andy soon, and, JJ, you will be seeing Dylan.'

Relieved at the news about Andy and Dylan, the other winners turned their minds back to the signs.

'The sevens,' mused Professor Abbass from behind his desk. 'I was just thinking about what they mean. Isabel and Mila, can you tell us again what you found?'

Isabel pointed at the triple sevens that surrounded each symbol they had recieved, in the HoloSpace. 'Seven, seven, seven.'

'Staring us in the face,' JJ said. 'How did I not see that?'

'None of us did,' Mila said. 'Just like we did not see that each countdown is twelve hours and fifty-seven minutes.'

No-one got the significance.

Isabel nodded for Mila to go on. 'This is seven hundred and seventy-seven minutes—seven, seven, seven, yes?'

Yasmin let out a gasp.

'We also found this,' Isabel said as she flicked the news story about the Spanish explosion into the HoloSpace. There, on the base of the destroyed statue, was the triple-seven symbol. 'This is where the symbol first appeared a week *before* the DARE Awards. Someone tried to blow up the National Library of Spain in Madrid.'

'It's definitely the same symbol,' Yasmin said. 'But why?'

Isabel shrugged. 'My guess is that the mastermind wanted us to discover this.'

'And?' Zander asked. 'Why sevens?'

The professor blew a sigh at the ceiling. 'Seven is considered by numerologists to be the most meaningful number there is. For most of history, humanity thought our world was built upon them.'

Seeing the DARE winners' frowning faces, the professor swept a hand towards the globe on his desk. '*Seven* continents. *Seven* seas. In the sky, ancient people saw *seven* celestial bodies with the naked eye—the Sun, Moon, Venus, Mercury, Mars, Jupiter, Saturn. That's why they named the *seven* days of the week after them—and they decided on a *seven*-day week because it's roughly the length of the *seven*-day phase of the moon. Then there are *seven* notes in music and everything we see is because of light that's made up of *seven* colours.'

The DARE winners traded looks. They hadn't realised how much the number could mean beyond Felix's obsession.

The professor continued. 'Because the ancients saw seven in the earth, the sea and the sky, they decided that seven had to represent ... perfection.'

'Perfection?' JJ asked with a laugh.

The professor nodded. 'Even today many people think seven is *the* "lucky" number.'

'Pah!' Isabel said. 'Nothing perfect or lucky about this.'

'There's not,' the professor agreed, 'but ... whoever's behind it might think they are doing something good.'

'Good?' Yasmin said. 'Hundreds of people are dead!'

The professor nodded. 'But, like history's worst villains, whoever's behind this could believe what they're doing is worth all the death and destruction.'

'Somehow that's worse,' JJ said, nervously.

The professor stood up, pacing excitedly behind his desk. 'Yes, yes,' he said to himself. 'I think I see it now.'

'See what?' Isabel asked impatiently.

'A method behind what we think is madness,' the professor said. 'Yesterday's attacks were on the Great Pyramid and the Suez Canal. The pyramid is one of the *Seven* Wonders of the Ancient World and the canal is considered by many as a wonder of the modern world.'

Realisation dawned on the DARE winners.

'No coincidence,' Yasmin said for all of them.

'No coincidence,' the professor agreed. 'I think we can assume the targets have symbolic meaning.'

Zander nodded. 'You said California, specifically Los Angeles, is known as "the car capital of the world".'

The professor nodded. 'But they weren't *just* cars. They were *AutoDrive* cars. Whoever is responsible might be saying handing power to machines is a recipe for disaster.'

'By actually creating a disaster?' Isabel said.

The professor sighed. 'These are only theories. Do you have any idea who's responsible and why you're involved?'

An awkard silence filled the office.

'You do suspect someone, don't you?' the professor pressed, wiping his forehead with a handkerchief. Then his eyes widened and his jaw dropped open. 'Oh, no, you don't think that . . . ?'

'There are seven of us,' said Zander softly.

'From seven continents,' Yasmin added.

'We got seven days to travel,' JJ offered.

'Felix is obsessed with sevens,' said Isabel.

'These attacks, they require much resources,' Mila said. 'Felix, he has the power.'

Samir slumped into his chair. 'But why would he do this?'

'We don't know,' Mila said softly.

'Actually, maybe we do,' Zander said. 'Maybe the targets are not just symbolic.'

All eyes were on him.

'Remember how the Egyptian attacks implicated technology produced by Felix's direct competitors?' he asked.

Isabel's eyes widened. 'Those news reports,' she said. 'It seemed like Infinity's AutoCars and AeroCars were unaffected by what just happened in California.'

Zander ran his hand through his thick black hair. 'And before I talked to Miss Chen outside about Andy and Dylan, she was on the phone answering a journalist's questions about that.' He shrugged, looking at each of them. 'Maybe Felix's plan is to make Infinity into more than a company. Maybe he wants to make it into a superpower.'

'What, so he can rule the world?' JJ asked.

The professor blinked rapidly. 'That's . . . insane.'

'Is it?' JJ pressed, face worried. 'When you talk about "history's worst villains", you're talking about people who tried to take over the world, aren't you?'

The professor gulped. 'Yes, yes . . . but *Felix Scott*?'

'I think we are moving too fast,' piped up Mila. 'Someone could be trying to make Felix look like he is to blame, yes?'

Zander nodded. 'True.' He lowered his voice. 'Andy and Dylan *did* seem to suspect Miss Chen was up to something.'

Yasmin quickly explained how Dylan and Andy had texted to say not to trust Felix's assistant.

'No matter who's behind this,' the professor began, 'what seems obvious about the signs is—'

But he was cut off by an incoming HoloSpace link. Andy and Dylan appeared. For the next few minutes, the boys described how they'd repeatedly escaped being smashed, drowned, burned and blown to pieces.

'All in all,' JJ said, 'you look in pretty good shape.'

Dylan nodded from the SpaceSkimmer whisking him to Seoul. 'I got a change of clothes and a new phone.'

'Yeah, me, too,' Andy said.

'Is your dad OK?' Yasmin asked softly.

Andy nodded. 'First call I made. He's . . . OK. Still in custody, but safe.' His eyes narrowed as he saw the Holo-Space windows containing the symbols, and he frowned at the professor. 'Sorry—we haven't been introduced.'

'Samir Abbass,' the academic replied. 'I'm a professor at the Library of Alexandria. I've been helping with the signs.'

Andy's face clouded with anger. 'We agreed we'd discuss it before telling anyone!'

Yasmin shifted in her chair. 'Andy, there wasn't time!'

'We were just trying to—' Zander said.

'To what?' Andy demanded.

'Find out if Colombia was really the target,' he shot back. 'Yasmin sent that warning text to you because of the professor's help.'

'We were trying to save your lives,' she said.

Andy blinked uncomfortably.

'It's OK, mate,' Dylan said. 'I mean, your dad knows, and President El Cerco knows. It's not like it's a secret-secret.'

The professor levelled his gaze at Andy. 'I promise whatever we discuss stays between us.'

'OK,' Andy demurred. 'I guess I'm just shaken up by . . .'

'By "everything", I think it is the word, yes?' Mila said.

Andy grinned. 'Yeah, that covers it.'

'We've got a lot to tell you,' said Dylan.

'Us, too,' said Isabel.

'Me, three,' said JJ with a grin.

Mila and Isabel filled Andy and Dylan in on what they'd discovered about the sevens, the countdown and the Madrid explosion.

Andy smacked a fist against his palm. 'This is ... crazy!'

Dylan nodded. 'It's off the scale, mate.'

But then Andy recounted how they'd found Ryder and how he'd been shot.

'Oh my, that is ...' Mila trailed off, eyes wide.

Dylan gulped. 'Horrible. It was horrible.' He decided against worrying them by mentioning he and Andy were probably suspects in Ryder's death. 'But we've seen worse since.'

'Before he died,' Andy continued, 'Ryder told us he was put up to hoaxing me by a woman who claimed to be an acting agent called "Kim Sher".'

'Ryder also said the woman claimed to be from Picture *Perfect* Agency and used the word *perfect* a few times,' Dylan added.

A shudder ran through them: they'd all heard Miss Chen use the word repeatedly.

'No such person, no such agency,' JJ said, eyes flitting behind his SmartGlasses.

'That's why you texted about Miss Chen!' Yasmin said.

'Precisely,' Andy said.

'Was there anything else?' Zander asked.

'Yeah,' Dylan said. 'Ryder thought the woman might be rich because of something he heard in the background.'

'But we never got a chance to find out more,' Andy said. 'That's when . . . he was shot.'

Zander shook his head in frustration.

'But there *is* something else,' Dylan sucked in a deep breath. 'I figured out that "Agent Kim Sher" is an alias. Just like "Agent M. Shrike". Same goes for "Games Thinker" and "Smear the King". They're all anagrams. They all contain the same letters as the name our enemy wants to be known by.'

No-one dared to breathe.

'It's us,' Dylan said, 'against "The Signmaker".'

'The Signmaker?' Yasmin whispered, her voice expressing the awe and fear they all felt.

'So many puzzles,' Isabel said. 'Games within games. He or she is playing with us!'

'OK, my turn for show and tell,' JJ said, eager to share the ChatAbout comment that had made him wonder. He flicked it into the HoloSpace.

This kid at my cousin's school was gonna win a DARE Award but got disqualified 'cos he cheated on his application
—*Luca Gabardi, 15, Pisa*

'If someone really did get busted cheating,' JJ said, 'then he or she might have a score to settle with Felix.'

Zander frowned. 'Wait, you believe this? It is probably someone trying to get a bit of fame for themselves.'

JJ's face reddened. 'It's a pretty serious accusation, though.'

Before JJ could say more, Zander turned his attention to Samir Abbass. 'Professor, you were going to say something about the signs before Andy and Dylan linked in. Will you tell us now?'

The professor nodded. The DARE winners watched in trembling silence as the academic got to his feet and pointed first to the sun symbol in the First Sign.

'The first attack occurred on "Sun-day", the beginning of the seven-day week. The second happened on "Moon-day". I expect we'll see this in the Third Sign.' He flicked a familiar symbol into the HoloSpace. 'You might have seen it a lot on bathroom doors, but did you know it's also the symbol for Tuesday?'

The horrible truth was suddenly all too clear.

Isabel nodded. 'Seven Signs.'

'Over seven days,' Zander added.

Mila shuddered. 'Means seven attacks!'

Seven attacks: those two words hung in the office and HoloSpace like the darkest of clouds.

Dylan broke the silence when he jumped up from his

seat in the SpaceSkimmer. 'I think I know how this works! There are seven of us from seven continents. Egypt was attacked. That's Africa. The United States was attacked. That's North America. So that's two DARE home countries and two continents.'

'Each attack will be on one of our countries!' Mila said.

'Maybe even our home cities, as well,' Dylan agreed. He glanced at JJ. 'Seoul, South Korea.' Next he looked at Isabel. 'Bogotá, Colombia.' Then Zander. 'Athens, Greece.' His eyes went to Mila. 'Chilean base, Antarctica.' Finally, he hooked a thumb at himself. 'Sydney, Australia.'

The DARE winners took a second for this to sink in. No-one protested. It fit perfectly with The Signmaker's obsession with sevens.

A new dread settled. What they saw now was the terrible scope of The Signmaker's plan, and how it threatened not just the world but each of them personally.

'Is there any chance we're wrong about this?' JJ asked.

Andy shrugged. 'Does anyone think we are?'

No-one did.

'Less than eleven hours until the Third Sign,' said Isabel. 'We have to use every second!'

'But we have no symbols to decode,' Yasmin said.

Mila pointed at the Madrid library news story in the HoloSpace. 'We can work on these clues, yes?'

Isabel's eyes held a steely determination. 'Mila's right,' she said. 'This Signmaker creep put those sevens there for a reason. We need to find out what it is!'

'You want to play The Signmaker's game?' Zander asked.

'What choice do we have?' Isabel replied. 'But I'd rather think of it as us *beating* him or her at the game.'

Andy nodded. 'That's the spirit. I think JJ's information is worth following up, too.'

JJ beamed, glad Andy was backing him.

'Really?' Zander sniffed. 'Seems likely it is no more than silly internet chatter.'

'Think about it,' JJ said. 'The DARE Awards are the opportunity of a lifetime. Fame, travel, Felix mentoring us and giving us a million bucks each. Someone who almost got what we have but lost it all? They'd have every reason to hate us and Felix.'

'But attacking Egypt and America because of a *grudge*?' Zander asked.

'Maybe if we're dealing with a psycho,' JJ shot back.

Isabel's eyes went from Zander to JJ. 'You've both got good points,' she said with uncharacteristic diplomacy. 'But even if it's a long shot, we should follow up this cheater, the Madrid bombing and any other clue we uncover.'

Zander shrugged. 'What do you suggest?' He pointed at the news story and the ChatAbout comment in the HoloSpace. 'We call this Detective Balboa in Madrid and this Luca Gabardi in Pisa and ask them what they know?'

Andy shook his head. 'Too much chance they'll shut us down by hanging up. We'll get more in person.'

'Like you did with Ryder?' Zander asked.

'Hey!' Andy said.

'Not cool, mate!' Dylan snapped defensively. 'That wasn't our fault!'

Zander held up his hands. 'Sorry, OK? But you *are* suggesting we go to Spain *and* Italy?'

'Well, what's your alternative plan, Z-man? You want us to just sit around and talk? In case you haven't noticed,' Andy said, 'you're the one who jumped a SpaceSkimmer to Egypt.'

'Exactly,' said JJ. 'We have the planes. Let's use them!'

'I say we vote,' Isabel said. 'Hands up if you think it's a good idea to go to Italy and Spain and investigate.'

She raised her hand. So did Mila. Andy and Dylan voted yes, followed by JJ and Yasmin.

Zander shook his head. 'I am not convinced. But as a Greek, I believe in democracy.'

'So, what're you saying, that you're in?' Andy asked.

'Which part of what I just said did you not understand?' Zander shot back. 'I am outvoted, six to one, so I will go along with this ... wild goose chase.'

'Hey, it's not—' JJ protested.

'Enough squabbling!' Isabel said. 'It's decided. Done. We're going. Now, does anyone have a plan?'

JJ took a deep breath, calming himself. 'Here's what I think,' he continued, flicking a world map up into the HoloSpace and pointing at Bogotá. 'Andy's SpaceSkimmer will be in Bogotá soon, right? Isabel and Mila, you get on it and the three of you go to Madrid and see what you can find out from Detective Balboa.' He turned the globe. 'Dylan, you pick me up'—his finger traced a line from Seoul to Alexandria and on to Pisa—'then we get Zander and Yasmin, and land in Pisa to find Luca Gabardi.'

Dylan laughed. 'You can tell your parents are travel agents.'

JJ chortled. 'It must've rubbed off.'

'Zander,' Isabel said, 'can you sort this out with Miss Chen?'

'Yes, she just loves me,' he said, unable to suppress a grin.

The professor cleared his throat. 'Can I come?' he asked. 'I'd like to help. I might be able to decode the Third Sign.'

Yasmin smiled. 'Yes, we—'

'I think we need to discuss this privately,' Andy said sternly. 'And decide together.'

The professor nodded. 'I understand. I'll go grab a drink.'

When he closed the door behind himself, Yasmin glared at Andy across the HoloSpace. 'That was so rude! Virtual or physical, we are all guests in the professor's office!'

Zander put a steadying hand on her arm. 'Andy clearly has issues.'

'My *issue* is that the professor is too eager to help,' Andy retorted. 'What would you do if you were him?'

'Call the authorities?' JJ said.

'Or maybe Felix,' Mila offered.

Andy nodded. '*Exactly* what he's not doing.'

'What, are you saying *he* is . . .' Zander's voice dropped. 'The Signmaker?'

Andy's face flushed a little. 'No, maybe—I don't know!' He held up fingers and counted them off. 'He knows all about symbols. He works in a library that has a huge amount of computing power as well as links to Felix. Why should he be above suspicion? He could be The Signmaker. Or a helper.'

Zander nodded. 'I hate to say this, but Andy makes some good points. The professor may not know Felix personally, but bringing him along is a bit risky.'

'You are both being paranoid, yes?' Mila said.

'Totally,' agreed Isabel. 'Zander and Yasmin contacted the professor. If they hadn't, he wouldn't be involved in this.'

'This is true,' Yasmin said. 'He is on our side. He helped us solve the Second Sign. Even if we did it too late.'

JJ nodded. 'Yup, I trust him.'

'I say we bring him,' Dylan agreed. 'If he *is* involved, watching him is the best way to find out. Like the saying goes, "Keep your friends close and your enemies closer".'

Andy shrugged at Zander. 'The one time I agree with you we're outvoted.'

Yasmin called the professor back to the office. 'We would love your help,' she said. 'But what can we tell Miss Chen?'

Samir Abbass's eyebrows arched mischievously. He crossed to a shelf of artefacts, picked up a fragment of stone tablet covered with hieroglyphs and handed it to Yasmin. 'Let's say you brought this to me. I think it's important and want to show it to a colleague in Pisa.'

Yasmin nodded. 'That should work.'

'Are you sure you want to do this?' Zander asked.

Samir smiled. 'I've always wanted to save the world.'

'You are going to tell your mother and father we are leaving, yes?' Mila asked.

'Not until we're in the air,' Isabel replied.

Mr and Mrs Garcia had gone to their jobs in downtown Bogotá, dropping Isabel's brother and sister off at school on the way. Like other citizens, they'd been reassured by President El Cerco's television appearance. The strongman leader had expressed condolences for the people of California but said life in Colombia had to carry on.

Mila's hugged her black cardigan uncertainly to her. 'You are serious?'

Isabel pushed her pink hair back with a headband and laced her boots up over the hems of her tie-dyed jeans. 'It's easier to say sorry later than risk being told no now.'

Her phone burbled as she shrugged her army-style green jacket on and threw her backpack over her shoulder.

'Good news,' she said, showing the text message to Mila.

> Cleared to fly SpaceSkimmer
> Bogotá–Madrid.
> Regards, Miss Chen.

Just in the last few minutes, the sounds of trouble had echoed from the barrio, and now a truck with riot police rumbled along the street. The air was bitter with smoke, and gunfire popped too close for comfort.

The phone chirped again with another text, this one from the Bogotá Cab Company.

'Typical,' grumbled Isabel. 'The driver's too scared to come closer,' she said. 'Probably thinks he'll be hit by a stray bullet.'

'What about *us*?' Mila asked.

'Just keep your head down and *run*,' said Isabel.

The girls hurried outside crouching low as they ran the fifty metres to the waiting taxi. Mila's heart was racing as Isabel threw open the door and leaped inside.

The taxi roared off, tyres pealing on the cobblestones.

'You should pay me danger money, coming to this neighbourhood,' complained the driver.

Isabel bit back her reply. She shouldn't judge the man too harshly. After President El Cerco's security crackdown and what had happened in California, the citizens of Colombia had every right to feel on edge. The talkback station on the taxi's radio wasn't helping. A caller was claiming that flying-saucer aliens had caused the events in the US and Egypt in preparation for their invasion of earth.

'I always say this would happen,' the taxi driver muttered.

'Aliens?' Isabel said.

'Not aliens.' He drummed his fingers against the steering wheel for emphasis. 'AutoDrive cars! I do not trust a computer to drive. These wheels are mine to control.' The driver tapped his temples. 'No-one can hack this old head.'

'Is that what you think happened?' Isabel said. 'A hack?'

'Someone on the radio said maybe it's one of these big honchos with their computers that makes these disasters happen.'

'A big honcho?' Mila asked.

'Señor Felix Scott,' the driver said. 'Very rich. These disasters make him richer.'

As the driver rattled on, Isabel and Mila traded a dark look. Theories about Felix were already out there, even without the world knowing about The Signmaker. Then again, he ranked alongside aliens as a possible culprit.

'I do not know,' the driver finished with a shrug. 'It is what the radio says.'

As they drove on, a new caller claimed the California carnage had been caused by a reversal of the earth's poles.

Isabel turned to smile at Mila. But she shuddered at what she saw out of the corner of her eye.

'Is everything OK?' Mila asked.

Isabel faced forward again. 'Yes, it's nothing.'

She hoped she was just being paranoid. But when she glanced back again a few minutes later, the black limousine she had spotted was still there in the rear window.

Mila smiled when she saw her phone light up with a text from her parents. 'Listen to this!' she said, laughing. 'A penguin escaped and wandered into my school!'

Isabel didn't reply.

'Should I tell them we're going to Madrid?' Mila said.

'But we're not!' said Isabel bluntly. 'Our flight is to

Cartagena—right here in Colombia. We go to Madrid tomorrow, silly!'

Mila's mouth fell open. But the look in Isabel's eyes stopped her from saying a word.

'Driver,' Isabel barked. 'My friend here made a mistake when she ordered the taxi. We need *domestic* departures today, not the international terminal.'

'You're the boss,' he said with a shrug. 'Hang on.'

Amid blaring horns, the driver swerved into the lane to the Domestic Departures terminal. El Dorado Airport's grey terminals and blue bunting rose out of lush gardens.

'Cartagena is so great,' Isabel said, eyes flitting past Mila's confused face to the taxi's rear window. 'It would have been a disaster if we'd missed the flight because you mixed up our schedule!'

Mila felt confusion and anger for being blamed for something she hadn't done. She started to turn round.

'Hey!' Isabel said, with a strained smile. 'Look at me.'

Now Mila understood. They were being followed! They had to leave this taxi driver with a false impression to help throw off their pursuers.

'I can't believe I got so mixed up,' Mila said. 'I would have been so sad if we had missed Cartagena!'

The cab stopped by the Domestic Departures sign. Isabel paid the driver and the girls got out.

'Who is following us?' Mila whispered.

'Black limo,' Isabel said softly. 'Over there.'

Mila glanced casually across the lanes of traffic. A

menacing dark vehicle was parked in a No Standing zone. A tinted window slid down to reveal a man with short platinum hair. The back doors opened and big guys in sunglasses and suits started climbing out.

'Let's go catch that plane!' Mila said through her fake smile. 'Cartagena, here we come!'

The girls made a beeline for the terminal. They saw a reflection of Mr Platinum and the sunglass-wearing suits behind him cutting between cars, zeroing in on the driver now idling in the taxi rank.

Isabel and Mila weaved through travellers to rush up an escalator into the main concourse. They passed passengers fretting beside trolleys stacked high with suitcases and staring anxiously up at departure boards. Barking announcements over the public-address system warned of delays because of the situation in the United States.

Isabel pointed at a crowd of teenagers beside a closed check-in counter. 'We have to blend in. Give those men the slip. Then head for the international terminal. Here, read this!' Isabel said, thrusting an airport map from a pamphlet stand into her friend's hands before she pushed deeper into the cluster of students.

Mila unfolded the map to the size of a small towel and ducked behind its layout of shops, food courts and gates. Her heart thudded faster after a risky glance over the map. Mr Platinum and his small army of suits were streaming off the escalator. They were coming straight for her!

'What am I going to do?' JJ asked his reflection in his bedroom mirror. Backpack over one shoulder, he looked sharp in his jeans, nano shirt and sneakers. He had everything he needed, except for his parents' permission to leave. 'Think, JJ,' he told himself, patting his black hair into its stylish swoop. 'You've got to come up with something.'

JJ could go downstairs, wake his mum and dad and tell them the Chairman had invited him to spend a few days at RoboWorld's Hotel. But that wouldn't explain why he had to leave a few hours before dawn—or why it was on the very day Dylan was due in Seoul.

Telling his parents the truth was even less appealing. JJ imagined explaining that he had to go to Italy because he and his friends had to save the world from a mysterious evil mastermind called The Signmaker, who'd orchestrated the deadly Egyptian and American attacks. Mr and Mrs Park would think their son had cracked under the pressure of doing school exams and being a DARE Awards winner.

JJ felt sick at what he'd have to do. Sneak out. Get to the SpaceSkimmer before his mum and dad knew he was gone. With them asleep, it shouldn't be too hard. When they woke up and found him gone—he'd have to worry about that later.

But when JJ inched open his bedroom door, his stomach plummeted. His parents were downstairs, talking softly.

JJ considered calling Dylan, telling him he couldn't get to the airport, that the SpaceSkimmer should just go on to Alexandria.

'No,' he said to himself. 'I can't do that. I have to . . .' *What?* He didn't know. But JJ crept down the stairs anyway.

The lounge room's wall screens were all on. But they weren't showing the horrible news about the carnage in California. Instead they were streaming night-vision video from the security cameras on the roof of the Park family home and along the high walls that protected the property.

'How did they find us?' JJ's mum was asking.

His dad shook his head. 'I knew it was a mistake to talk to the journalists.'

Guilt stabbed JJ in the stomach. He was the one who had encouraged his parents to give interviews after reporters turned up outside their house.

'Sorry,' he said, stepping off the stairs.

Mr and Mrs Park spun round.

'JJ, why are you up so early?' his father said.

'And already dressed?' his mother added.

JJ joined them by the screens. 'Are those more journalists out there?'

'Yes,' Mr Park said. 'Yes, that's right.'

JJ peered at the security feed. A man sat in the front seat of a van and another shadowy shape loitered at a pavilion table. There was a third figure beneath a banyan tree.

'Well,' JJ chuckled, 'let 'em sit out there in the cold.'

His parents nodded, but JJ felt the anxiety coming off

them like a bad smell.

Mrs Park's brow furrowed at the backpack on his shoulder. 'Son, what is this?'

JJ fought panic and made the snap decision to bend the truth. 'I've been talking to Dylan, and his mum and dad are filming in Italy and they asked if we'd like to join them for a day. Dylan's SpaceSkimmer lands soon and I was hoping I could join him. Yasmin and Zander are going to be there and my exams are finished and I've done everything you asked and it'd only be for a day and then we'd come right back and . . .'

JJ forced himself to stop babbling. 'I was going to wake you up and ask, but then I saw you were already awake doing . . . whatever it is you're doing.'

A look passed between his parents. JJ had the idea they weren't telling him everything. It made him feel less bad about holding back things from them.

'Son,' his dad said, 'you wait here. Your mother and I need to talk.'

While his parents murmured in the kitchen, JJ played around with the surveillance screens. Zooming in showed that the guy in the pavilion was checking out their house with night-vision binoculars. The driver in the van was talking to someone on a mobile phone. But the third man was nowhere to be seen.

JJ's blood went icy. Maybe the men out there weren't media! Maybe they were minions sent by The Signmaker. JJ shook off his fear. No! It didn't make sense. They had to be reporters, like his parents said. But something about them wasn't right. He just wasn't sure what it was.

Mr and Mrs Park returned from the kitchen.

'Son,' said his dad, 'we don't think it's a good idea—'

JJ's stomach lurched. They weren't going to let him go. He should've climbed out the window!

'—for you to be here right now. So yes, you can go with Dylan.'

'Really?!' JJ said.

'We, ah, don't want you to be subjected to this kind of, um, media harassment,' his mum said.

Mr Park pointed to the screen. 'The alley behind our house looks clear. Go out that way. Get to the corner and hide. We'll call a taxi.'

'Hang on,' JJ said. 'Can't I just go out the front? Tell them off for being snoops and bullies? I mean—'

His mother shook her head. 'That will just encourage them. We tried it your way. Now you do it ours—or you don't go anywhere with Dylan.'

JJ held up his hands. 'OK, OK.'

'When we see the taxi approach,' Mr Park said, 'we'll make sure there's a diversion.'

'Diversion?' JJ asked.

His dad allowed himself a smile. 'Son, do you mind if I raid your old toy box?'

Mr Platinum and his suits milled at the edge of the crowd of college students.

'Next flight to Cartagena's not for forty minutes from gate seventeen,' he barked, pointing at an overhead departure board. 'They could be anywhere. Spread out. Find them!'

Mila buried her nose in her map as one of the men pushed his way into the crowd. Her heart pumped wildly, her hands shook and her clothes were wet with cold sweat. Who were these men? What did they want? What were they going to do to her? Any second now this goon would push down the flimsy map that was no hiding place at all. Mila wanted to scream.

A nasally American voice pierced the airport's hum.

'No! Like, *you* listen to *me*, Mason!' the girl screeched. 'Don't you dare, like, tell me nothing happened! I saw you kiss Whitney, OK, with my very own eyes!' The girl let out a dramatic sob. 'But I *love* you!'

Uncomfortable laughter rippled through the crowd.

'How embarrassing!' chuckled a student near Mila.

'Totes awkward!' her friend agreed.

Mila risked a glance up from her map. Inches away, the man in the suit had scrunched his mouth up in distaste as he looked in the direction of the commotion.

'Mason—I love you!' The girl's outburst was louder. 'Please just talk to me, baby!'

Shaking his head, the man in the suit shuffled away, seemingly determined to search a less embarrassing part of the airport.

Mila let herself breathe—and then nearly fell over when the crowd parted to reveal the girl making all the kerfuffle was ... Isabel!

The DARE winner had ditched her chunky bracelets, tucked her pink hair under a beanie, donned her sunglasses and wrapped her jacket around her waist.

Mila risked a look at the suit. He was farther up the concourse and shaking his head at Mr Platinum as they walked to the next departure gate.

Isabel sauntered over with a cheeky smile, winking as she dipped her sunglasses.

'You're ... mad,' Mila said.

'Nothing like hiding out in the open,' Isabel said. 'No-one expects that.'

'It's lucky he went away when he did, yes?' Mila said.

'Because he was about to find you?'

'Because I was about to *die*—of embarrassment for you!'

The girls headed for the shuttle that transported passengers from the domestic to the international terminal.

'Who were those men?' Mila said when they reached the far end of the platform.

Isabel shrugged. 'My guess is—'

Her phone rang and the caller ID showed: David Imanez.

'Speak of the devil,' she said. 'Accept call. Señor Imanez,' Isabel said, Mila standing close so she could listen. 'So nice to hear from you.'

'Call me David,' he replied. 'How are you and Mila?'

'Hmm, kinda busy.'

'Can I see you?'

'My hair's a mess,' Isabel said. 'Not a good look for a video call.'

Mila stifled a giggle.

'I mean,' he said, 'can I come and pick you and Mila up? President El Cerco wants to meet with you both.'

Isabel scoffed. 'We're supposed to believe you now?'

'I'm sorry I had to trick you,' David said coolly. 'But this time it's different. It's obvious you two have a direct line to whoever's behind what happened in California. I'll ... I'll—'

'You'll what?' Isabel said.

'I'll send a car.'

'You mean *another* car?' Isabel said.

'What?'

'Limo. Platinum-haired guy leading a bunch of men in black suits?'

David paused. 'I don't know what you're talking about.'

'Don't pretend,' Isabel said sharply. 'They just—'

Mila stepped back and shook her head. Isabel realised that if David *hadn't* sent Mr Platinum, then she shouldn't give away their real location. If he knew they were at the airport, he could cancel their passports and ground their SpaceSkimmer.

'Just what?' David prompted. 'What car? What men?'

'Oh, come on,' Isabel said. 'The guys parked across from my house right now.'

'They're not ours,' David said.

'Really?' Isabel said in a small voice, throwing in a gulp for good measure.

'Really!' David shot back. 'Stay inside. I'll be there in ten minutes!'

'OK,' she replied. 'Hurry.' Isabel hung up as the airport shuttle raced into the station. 'Was it wrong to lie?' she asked as they squeezed into a crowded carriage.

Mila shook her head. 'We have no reason to trust David.'

Isabel bit her lip. 'You're right. But if he didn't send Mr Platinum and his men, then who did?'

Mila almost didn't dare to say it. 'Could it be "the you-know-who"?' she asked softly.

A shiver danced through Isabel.

JJ crept through his backyard, palm fronds reaching out from the darkness like skeletal fingers. He ducked down along the shadowy pebble path, grabbed the rear gate's latch, swung it open as quietly as he could and poked his head through to peer along the dark laneway.

Heart thumping, breath caught in his throat, JJ jumped back into the safety of the shadows.

A hulking figure lurked under a streetlight at the end of the block! The third man was watching the alley!

'Damn,' JJ whispered to himself. He wondered why all of a sudden the media had turned so aggressive. His parents weren't *that* interesting, and he'd already given interviews to anyone who asked.

Elbows resting on his knees, JJ crouched and considered his situation. He had to get away quickly. But he would be seen as soon as he stepped into the alley.

He tapped his fingers against the hard plastic and steel casing of his legs and looked up at the tall concrete walls that enclosed his yard. All the properties on this block were separated by these big barriers. They were too high and sheer to climb but . . . he could jump!

JJ knew his robotic leg power could thrust him high enough to land on top of the wall. He'd jumped as high as five metres in the park, his landing cushioned by the coil-spring tech built into his feet and calves. If he could get up onto the wall, then he could leapfrog across that yard to the next wall. Five jumps like that and he'd be at the corner. He gazed up, working out angles and velocities, adjusting for the weight of his backpack. His thoughts became electrical impulses that flashed commands to processors which controlled the springs, cables and motors in his powerful legs. His mind, body and the robotic leg mecha he'd designed were one seamless system and made him far more physically powerful than the average human could be. He took a deep breath to calm himself. Then another.

JJ was scared. He could do this in theory. But he also pictured what would happen if he miscalculated, missed the top of a wall, and smashed down into a backyard. All the leg mecha in the world couldn't defy gravity or the injuries he might suffer.

'Come on,' he whispered to himself. 'One small step for JJ, one giant leap for mankind.'

JJ sprang into the air.

He arced up through the night and landed in a crouch on top of the wall with his arms outstretched. He swayed, over-balancing. His neighbour's greenhouse was right beneath him, ready to slice him to ribbons if he fell into its glass roof.

JJ steadied and stilled himself. He glanced over his shoulder. The man under the streetlight was still looking straight down the alley. 'So long, sucker,' JJ said under his breath, and leaped away.

Moments later, he dropped off the final wall, landing

gently in the grass by the sidewalk. He scrambled to the corner and took cover in some bushes.

Peering into the darkened park, he saw the man from the van was now huddled with the other man outside the pavilion. The duo turned, faces lit up by headlights, as the taxi approached. If JJ emerged from the bushes now, he'd be spotted for sure.

'Come on, Mum and Dad,' he hissed to himself. 'Where's that diversion?'

Suddenly the air over the park blazed with rainbow lights and blared with tinny K-pop music. The men shouted as they swatted at JJ's old UFO and quadchopper drones, which zoomed around them crazily, ducking and diving, blinding and deafening.

JJ scrambled from the bushes and jumped into the slowing taxi. 'Incheon Airport,' he said, ducking down in the back seat. 'Infinity Air terminal.'

As the taxi merged onto the freeway, JJ couldn't resist a look back at the flashing drones still harassing the reporters. He laughed with new-found respect for his parents. Who knew they could be so cool and resourceful? But then JJ realised what didn't make sense about the men staking out his house. The thought troubled him all the way to the airport. If the trio outside his house were media people, then where were their camera and sound equipment?

The girls joined the river of people on the platform and rode the escalator up into the terminal. Standing on a higher step, Mila turned and looked back at Isabel.

'Maybe The Signmaker didn't send them. Maybe they are criminals angry because of your Books not Guns cam—'

Mila's eyes widened and she turned round quickly.

'What?' Isabel whispered. 'What is it?'

'Mr Platinum and his men,' Mila hissed. 'Down there. Behind us!'

The girls stood frozen in fear, wedged by the crowd on the escalator now taking forever to reach the concourse.

Mila leaned back to Isabel. 'When we get to the top,' she whispered, 'do we try to blend in again?'

'Uh-uh,' her friend answered as the escalator levelled out. 'Now . . . we run like hell!'

The girls sprang off the metal landing and raced into the international terminal.

'Get out of the way!' Isabel yelled as she rushed between annoyed passengers. 'Flight to catch!'

Mila glanced over her shoulder. Mr Platinum and the suits had seen them! They were pushing people aside at the top of the escalator.

Arms and legs blurring, backpacks jostling, the girls belted through the crowds. As they closed in on the Infinity

Air departure gate, they saw Andy at the security barrier beside an armed guard. His waving hand dropped and his eyes widened as he saw the men chasing after them.

Andy scrambled from the gate. In a fluid motion, he tore a stacked luggage trolley from the grip of a startled tourist. One leg kicking frantically, Andy used it like a scooter, hurtling straight for Isabel and Mila.

'Out of the way!' he shouted.

The girls split and streaked past on either side of him.

Andy leaped clear as the moving mountain of suitcases ploughed into Mr Platinum and his men and scattered them like bowling pins.

Skidding to a stop, Andy pumped his fist. 'St-rrrike!' Then he turned and raced back to the gate, where the guard was ushering Isabel and Mila into the safety of the terminal.

Andy caught up as they hurried to the SpaceSkimmer. 'Who were your friends?' he panted.

'We don't know,' Isabel said, equally breathless. 'But wow, what you just did, it was—'

'Gnarly? I think this is the word,' Mila gasped.

They burst into laughter.

'So, this is Bogotá?' Andy said. 'I like it already.'

'You're not seeing it at its best,' Isabel said, glancing back in case Mr Platinum and his suits came rushing up the corridor.

'Perhaps another time?' Andy said.

'I'm going to hold you to that,' Isabel said. 'But right now let's get out of here!'

'That's the SpaceSkimmer,' Infinity's terminal steward said, leading JJ into the VIP lounge. He pointed out the window to where the gleaming aircraft sat waiting. With its swept-back wings, silver fuselage and bulbous thrusters, and rear rocket, the aircraft looked like a sleek spacecraft from some future civilisation.

JJ smiled. Despite everything, he couldn't help being excited about taking his first sub-orbital flight.

The steward walked over to one of the plush sofas that lined the area. 'And here is your friend,' he said, giving Dylan a gentle shake. Dylan sat up, blinking and bleary-eyed.

'JJ,' he said groggily. 'Mate, how are you?'

'I feel how you look.' The adrenalin of escaping his house had worn off, leaving JJ exhausted.

'Can't believe I fell asleep,' Dylan said. 'Guess I must've needed it.'

'We all need about a million hours' shut-eye.' JJ yawned.

Dylan walked over to the door to the lounge and put one foot outside.

JJ watched, bemused. 'What are you doing?'

'I want to say I've at least set foot in South Korea,' Dylan said with a smile. 'But I am bummed out that I'm not going to meet RoboJJ.'

JJ did a stiff robotic-style swivel with his arms held out

at stiff angles. 'Who says you haven't already?'

Dylan guffawed. 'Good point. How *can* I tell if it's the real you?'

'Do droids do this?' JJ roared out a big burp.

Dylan fanned the air with his hand. 'Mate, gross!'

Captain Danny Hunt appeared in the SpaceSkimmer's doorway. 'Are you two jokers ready for take-off?'

The boys took their seats and the flight attendant strapped them in.

JJ checked the Games Thinker website on his phone.

06:57:00

He looked across at Dylan and saw him doing the same thing.

Time was running out.

The SpaceSkimmer taxied along the runway and then picked up speed.

Dylan looked at JJ across the aisle.

'Whatever else happens today,' he said, 'you're gonna love this.'

JJ's smile said he already did.

They roared off into the sky.

The Signmaker

The giant HoloSpace showed the SpaceSkimmers in flight, one zooming west away from Seoul and the other flashing through the skies over north-east Venezuela. The DARE winners were all headed for Europe, getting closer to the next target. Not that they knew it yet.

Leaning back in an expensive leather chair, The Signmaker grinned in the golden glow of the lair's over-head lights. The game was getting more intriguing as new challenges emerged. Although the mastermind had wanted the DARE winners to eventually find the news story about the Madrid library bomb blast, JJ stumbling across those ChatAbout comments from Luca Gabardi in Pisa had been a complete surprise. Even with The Signmaker's vast computing power, it wasn't possible to monitor every nook and cranny of the internet. If the DARE winners got to Pisa, they might pose a threat to the plan. But, The Signmaker realised, it also presented the chance to weave a new web ...

The Signmaker smiled. This was like a vast chess game. The DARE winners were making their moves. The Signmaker had to always be two or three moves ahead. But the next play would remove a piece from the board.

A HoloSpace window showed satellite video of the professor's beaten-up old Ford pulling up outside his apartment building in Alexandria's garment district. The visit to the professor had served its secret purpose as part of the plan's endgame. But now the professor had no further role to play. He was just in the way. The Signmaker watched as the satellite feed showed him walking into his apartment building's entrance. He was there to say goodbye to his family before he headed to the Alexandria airport to join the others.

Goodbye was right.

The Signmaker uttered a series of commands that became encrypted data flashed securely via satellite to its destination.

Seconds later, the simple response appeared on the HoloSpace.

DIRECTIVES RECEIVED.

First Alexandria, then Pisa.

Loose ends needed to be tied up.

The SpaceSkimmer shot through the upper atmosphere towards Europe.

'Wow!' Isabel exclaimed in the InvisiLounge.

Even though they'd experienced it before, Mila and Andy were just as awed by the breathtaking view offered by the plane's nano-engineered transparent fuselage. To their right were the green mountains, blue waters and yellow sand of the coasts of Guyana, Suriname and French Guiana. To their left was the Caribbean Sea, an aquamarine expanse dotted with the islands of Grenada, Barbados and St Lucia. On the arc of the horizon, they could just make out Puerto Rico rising from the haze. But it wasn't long before the Atlantic Ocean darkened ahead of them as the SpaceSkimmer closed in on night across the time zones.

Andy, Isabel and Mila watched a HoloSpace newsfeed of President El Cerco giving a press conference.

'That guy standing behind the president is David Imanez,' Isabel said to Andy.

'He doesn't look happy,' Andy said. 'Maybe you should text him a smiley face?'

Isabel laughed. Just after the SpaceSkimmer took off, she had received a barrage of texts from David. At first the messages had been confused. Why weren't she and Mila at Isabel's house? Then they became furious. How dare they leave the country! Isabel simply hadn't replied.

Now another text burbled on her phone.

'Him again?' Mila said.

Isabel shook her head. 'Miss Chen. She's arranged a car to pick us up and take us to the Infinity Hotel in Madrid.'

'Is that what we want to do?' Andy asked.

Isabel shrugged. 'It's going to be late when we get to Spain. But if we're lucky, Detective Balboa might work the night shift.'

It took a few minutes for her to find the number for Madrid's police headquarters. When she called she was told Detective Balboa had left for the day but that he'd be back in the office at eight tomorrow morning.

'That's too late,' Andy said. 'We can't wait that long.'

Isabel nodded. 'We need to find him. But how?'

'Hugo Balboa, yes?' Mila said, frowning as she swiped at her phone.

'What're you doing?' Andy asked.

'Playing a hunch—this is what it is called, yes?'

Isabel raised her eyebrows. 'Well?'

'Aha, OK,' said Mila, smiling. 'Hugo R. Balboa. 3/1212 Calle de Alcala.'

'What's that?' Andy asked.

'It is his home address,' said Mila, showing him and Isabel her phone's screen. '*White Pages Madrid*. Sometimes the simple answer it is the best. They have only one Hugo Balboa listed. Perhaps a visit, yes?'

'In the middle of the night?' Isabel asked.

'What choice do we have?' Andy said. 'Besides, I know how to talk to cops. If he thinks we've got info about the bombing, he won't be able to resist talking to us.'

The SpaceSkimmer touched down in Madrid, and Andy, Isabel and Mila quickly cleared customs and jumped into a waiting Infinity car.

'Infinity Hotel?' the driver asked.

Isabel told him no. Twenty minutes later, their driver was whizzing them along a tree-lined street of shops and apartments. 'This is it,' he said. '1212 Calle de Alcala.'

Andy, Mila and Isabel peered out at a narrow door between a florist and a bookshop.

'Wait for us around the corner, will you, driver?' Isabel asked.

The trio got out of the car and stood on the footpath.

'So, what do we do?' Isabel asked.

'Leave it to me,' Andy said. He pressed the buzzer next to the door marked 'H. Balboa'.

A second later static crackled from the intercom's speaker. '*Que*?' a voice barked.

'Detective Balboa?' Andy said. 'I need to see you.'

'Who is this?'

'My name is Andy Freeman. I'm from the United States. It's about the library bombing. It's urgent.'

'OK.' A grunt crackled from the intercom. 'Stay there.'

Andy grinned at the girls.

'Cops are the same wherever you go,' he said. 'They can't resist the idea of cracking a cold case.'

The door buzzed open and suddenly they were staring down the muzzle of a gun. Andy yelped. Isabel let out a cry. Mila put her hands up.

The stocky man holding the gun had a brutish face, chomped a foul-smelling cigar and was a ball of muscle wearing a singlet and tracksuit pants. Detective Hugo Balboa looked like he lived at the gym—and liked nothing better than breaking bad guys in half. His fierce eyes went from Andy to Isabel to Mila. 'You're kids,' he spat. 'What're you doing, coming to my place in the middle of the night?'

'Y-y-your name, it was in the *White Pages*,' Andy managed.

'That's not an invitation for midnight visits!' Balboa grunted.

'We just want to talk,' Isabel protested.

'So talk,' he growled, lowering the gun and tucking it into the waistband of his tracksuit pants. 'You've got information about the bombing?'

Andy nodded. 'Not exactly. You see, we're the DARE Award winners—'

'I don't care if you're Oscar winners,' Balboa barked. 'If you haven't got information for me, then get out of my face and away from my place.'

'Detective,' Isabel said firmly, 'we're investigating the bombing. We've come a long way to see you. We need to know what you know about the suspects, the explosive, anything that wasn't in the newspaper.'

'Oh, you do, do you?' Balboa said with a menacing grin.

'You want *me* to tell *you* what *I* know? Five seconds to clear out before I arrest you. *Cinco, cuatro . . .*'

Andy saw red. He stepped forward. He knew a few choice insults in Spanish. This was the perfect opportunity to let them fly. But before he could open his mouth, Mila had him by the arms and was pulling him away.

'We're going,' Isabel said as they retreated. 'Sorry to disturb you, Detective.'

The trio rounded the corner and stopped under a street-light half a block from the waiting car.

'That went well, yes?' Mila said.

'You sure do know how to talk to cops,' Isabel said.

'It wasn't like you did any better,' Andy shot back.

'So, what now?' she asked. 'Do we try him again?'

'No need!' Mila blurted. 'There *is* someone else we can ask!' She held up her phone showing the *Madrid Sentinel* story about the explosion at the National Library. 'Look. It says "By a staff reporter". They haven't got robojournalists yet, have they?'

Andy shook his head. 'Not until JJ invents one.'

Mila ignored his joke. 'Whoever wrote this article could know more, yes?'

'You're right!' Isabel said. 'Great idea.'

Andy grinned at Mila. 'When I met you I thought you were a bit shy, maybe even a little weird,' he said. 'Now I think you're a bit weird . . . but totally brilliant!'

The car sped along the wide road that curved along Alexandria's waterfront, the moon hanging fat and yellow over the Mediterranean.

'Yes, you can leave your car at the Infinity Air terminal,' Miss Chen was saying into her SmartGlasses in the car's shotgun seat. 'No, Professor, the SpaceSkimmer will not take off without you. OK, goodbye.'

She turned to Zander and Yasmin in the back seat. 'Why the sudden interest in Italy from you and the professor?'

'JJ got a message from a boy in Italy who's really sick,' Zander said, launching into the cover story he and Yasmin had quickly devised at the hotel before leaving. 'His big wish is to meet JJ. So JJ said he wanted to go and surprise him.'

'We thought it'd be nice to go, too,' Yasmin chimed in. 'That way he gets four DARE winners for the price of one.'

Miss Chen nodded. 'We really should tell Infinity Media about this.'

'What?' Yasmin said.

'This could be very positive publicity for the DARE Awards. I will reach out to our public relations manager to arrange something.'

Yasmin tried to control her panic. Their cover story wouldn't withstand scrutiny.

'Miss Chen,' she said, 'JJ said he really wanted to keep this private. Apparently, the boy is . . .'

'Is?' she prompted.

'Not expected to live long.'

Miss Chen blinked. 'I see. That is sad. Very well. I understand.' She tilted her head quizzically. 'About the professor, why could he not show the artefact to his colleague via HoloSpace?'

Yasmin tensed but Zander let out an unfazed chuckle. 'We think the professor just wants an excuse to ride a SpaceSkimmer.'

Miss Chen took this in. 'It is quite the experience.' She thought for a moment and frowned slightly. 'Why did Isabel and Mila and Andy decide to go to Spain?'

Yasmin swallowed hard. They hadn't prepared for this— and now it sounded like Miss Chen was suspicious.

But Zander didn't miss a beat.

'You know much Isabel loves her art?' he said. 'She heard about some exhibition opening tomorrow morning and convinced Mila and Andy it was a once-in-a-lifetime opportunity.'

Miss Chen's expression was cryptic. If she was The Signmaker, she knew they were lying about all of it. Was she playing with them? Her cold manner made it impossible to tell. 'I see,' was all she said, facing forward again.

'Will the SpaceSkimmers be on standby at Pisa and Madrid airports?' Zander probed.

Miss Chen nodded. 'Just as you asked. Will you be going

back to your scheduled destinations?'

Zander and Yasmin swapped a glance. There was no way to tell where they'd have to go next, only that it'd be one of their home countries—that's if Dylan's theory was right.

'Not sure,' Yasmin said cheerfully. 'We thought we might decide that together.'

'When else are we going to have the chance to travel like this?' Zander said. 'The SpaceSkimmers are so amazing, I would be happy just flying around for the rest of my life!'

Miss Chen tapped at her tablet. 'I have advised Captains Hunt and Demelo to fly where you tell them. That way you can liaise with them directly.' She offered a rare smile. 'Felix will be glad you are making the most of your prizes. I will update him on your movements.'

Yasmin flashed a fearful glance at Zander.

'Update him?' she mouthed.

Everything about Miss Chen—her aloof expressions, the words she used, her calm tone of voice—made her seem somehow sinister.

Zander slipped on his SmartGlasses. Yasmin pushed closer to him on the back seat.

'What're you doing?' she whispered as his eyes flitted.

'Messaging the others,' he whispered, 'so our stories match up.'

Alexandria's Bourg El-Arab Airport shone in a crown of yellow lights against the dark desert. The car took a side road and went through security checks to drive directly up to the boarding area.

The driver stopped the car outside the Infinity Air terminal. JJ and Dylan bounded from the building's glass doors as Zander and Yasmin jumped out of the vehicle to greet them in a flurry of hugs and handshakes. 'I will say goodbye,' Miss Chen said, standing stiffly by the car. 'I have business to take care of here in Alexandria. I hope your visit with the sick boy goes well. What was his name again?'

'Luca Gabardi,' JJ blurted before he could stop himself.

Miss Chen looked like she was filing the information away. 'We will be sure to send him something special on behalf of Felix and Infinity,' she said as she climbed back into the vehicle. 'Safe travels.'

Miss Chen nodded at the driver, her window slid up, and the car headed back out of the airport.

'What was that?' Yasmin said. 'Do you think she suspects?'

Zander grimaced. 'I hope not.'

Yasmin shivered. 'She's creepy. Even if she's totally innocent, I'm so glad she's not coming.'

'Double definitely,' said Dylan. 'Let's get on the plane, yeah?'

They walked across the tarmac.

A horn beeped as they climbed the metal stairs to the SpaceSkimmer's doorway. Everyone turned to look at the beaten-up Ford stopping by the security gate.

'Is that the professor?' asked JJ.

'Must be,' Zander replied.

The Infinity security guard waved the vehicle through. The Ford chugged along the entrance road.

'Now I am glad *he's* coming,' Yasmin said.

The others nodded as the professor approached. They could see him behind the wheel, afro silhouetted against the airport's lights. He raised a hand from the steering wheel as he headed for the terminal.

Dylan glanced up from the Games Thinker website on his phone. 'Only six-and-a-half hours till the Third Sign. I hope the professor's help means we can—'

KABOOM!

The Ford exploded up off the road in a roaring flash. The world seemed to be nothing but heat and light and noise. The DARE winners screamed as the shock wave sent them sprawling, slamming them into the SpaceSkimmer stairs. Everything happened at once. Inside the car the professor's shadow was eclipsed by a white-hot fireball. The little Ford was like a supernova, shooting flame in every direction. Another explosion shattered the vehicle as its fuel tank detonated. The car spun violently into the air, flipped end over end and then smashed back into the tarmac with a sickening crunch.

Dylan jumped up from where he'd been thrown to the tarmac. He started to run towards the burning wreckage.

'No!' yelled JJ. 'Don't!'

With a huge leap off the SpaceSkimmer stairs, JJ raced after Dylan. He jumped and—

Krrafoompa!

What was left of the professor's car disintegrated with a thunder crack and became a blazing storm of shredding metal and shattering glass. Debris pinged off the SpaceSkimmer's wings and fuselage.

'Ahh!' cried Zander as a piece of hot shrapnel sliced into his shoulder.

Yasmin saw him clamp a hand to his bloody shirt.

'I'm OK!' he yelled.

She whirled. Amid the smoke and debris, Dylan and JJ were unmoving on the tarmac.

They were dead. Yasmin was sure of it. They'd been killed by shrapnel as fast and lethal as bullets. She unleashed a soul-piercing wail and fell back against the SpaceSkimmer stairs.

Yasmin sobbed—with relief.

Out on the tarmac, Dylan and JJ stirred, faces craning up to check on each other and what was left of the Ford.

Her friends were alive! JJ had tackled Dylan to the ground a split second before the final explosion.

But the professor's vehicle was like a horrible flower that had opened twisted orange and black petals to the night sky.

'I have to—' Yasmin gasped, starting down the stairs. 'The professor, he—'

Zander grabbed her arm. 'No,' he said forcefully. 'There is nothing you can—'

'Y'all get on the plane!' a voice commanded.

Captain Danny Hunt stood above Yasmin and Zander in the SpaceSkimmer's doorway, a .45 pistol held double-handed, his scarred face set with an expression of pure determination.

'Now!' he yelled, taking the stairs three at a time as he rushed down past Yasmin and Zander. 'Move!'

Jumping onto the tarmac, Hunt landed with a roll and came up into a shooting stance to cover Dylan and JJ.

'Boys!' he yelled. 'Get your butts on that plane! Pronto!'

He aimed the pistol past them, covering the wreck, sweeping the weapon left and right.

Dylan and JJ picked themselves up and groggily ran for their lives.

Yasmin was first into the SpaceSkimmer.

'This way!' the panicked flight attendant said, pointing urgently to a seat. She turned to Zander, Dylan and JJ and ushered them inside. 'Hurry!'

There was a *thump-thump-thump* as Captain Danny Hunt raced up the stairs and dived into the plane.

'Prepare for urgent take-off!' he told the flight attendant.

'Captain,' Dylan yelled, voice straining. 'The professor, shouldn't we—'

'He's gone!' the pilot yelled. With a push of a button, he sent the robostairs rolling away and closed the SpaceSkimmer door. 'We don't know what blew him up! Could be a drone. Someone with a launcher. We gotta get outta here!'

Yasmin wiped tears from her cheeks. 'We can't just leave him.'

'He's dead,' shouted Captain Hunt. 'We could be next!'

JJ gulped. 'Is the plane damaged?'

If shrapnel had punctured the SpaceSkimmer's fuselage, it could come apart in the upper atmosphere and burn back to earth like a falling star.

'No choice but to find out,' the pilot said, rushing into the cockpit. 'Right now, we're safer in the air than on the ground! Strap yourselves in!'

Hearts thumping, the DARE winners gripped their seat rests with white knuckles. The seconds stretched as the

SpaceSkimmer's engines powered up.

Dylan tried to swallow. His mouth was too dry.

The SpaceSkimmer lurched forward, throwing the flight attendant off balance. She quickly strapped in as the plane sped down the runway like a racing car, pressing everyone back into their seats. The world blurred through the windows as the SpaceSkimmer lifted off, shot into the sky and climbed steeply.

JJ groaned. Dylan's eyes bulged.

The SpaceSkimmer's displays showed it making a forty-five-degree ascent and already going faster than the speed of sound.

Straining up from her seat, Yasmin peered through the window and saw Alexandria's lights dwindling against the expanse of dark desert and sea. The heaviness pressing against her heart was more than just the pressure of the g-forces. She was leaving behind an Egypt in crisis. And down there, the professor was—

She screamed as the SpaceSkimmer dropped in turbulence that threw everyone hard up against their harnesses.

As he was slammed back into his seat, Dylan grabbed a sick bag and threw up loudly.

The SpaceSkimmer angled upward more acutely, gaining even more speed.

JJ's groans grew louder. His eyes were wide with fear.

Yasmin gasped. All the blood drained from her face.

Zander's jaw was clenched as tight as his grip on the seat rests.

The displays showed why the SpaceSkimmer was shuddering, shaking, straining.

$$ALTITUDE: 55,000\ METRES$$
$$ANGLE: 60\ DEGREES$$
$$SPEED: 4,000\ KILOMETRES/HOUR$$

'Is this normal?' Yasmin shouted.

Zander could barely shake his head for the g-forces. 'Faster ... steeper ... than ... before,' he said.

The SpaceSkimmer slowed, straightened, sending the DARE winners floating up in their harnesses. They hung there a moment and then settled as gravity pulled them back to their seats.

'Uggggh!' JJ frantically grabbed his seat-back sick bag, just getting it to his face in time to catch a torrent of vomit.

'Sorry,' he muttered.

Gradually the plane levelled out, the angle winding back to zero as they reached a cruising altitude of seventy-five thousand metres.

Captain Hunt appeared in the cabin.

'The SpaceSkimmer's on autopilot,' he said. 'It's OK for a few minutes. Is everybody all right?'

They nodded numbly.

'We're already a hundred clicks from Alexandria,' he said. 'So we should be safe now.'

'Should be?' JJ asked.

'If your friend was taken out with a space-based laser,'

Captain Hunt said, 'then we're still totally vulnerable if the satellite's orbit gives it a clear shot. Except...'

'Except?' asked Zander.

'If that was the case,' Captain Hunt said, 'we'd all be dead like...your friend.'

Dylan, Zander, JJ and Yasmin flinched.

The professor—eccentric, friendly, brilliant, helpful—had been so full of life. He'd just been trying to help. He'd had a wife and kids. Now he was dead. Blown to a billion pieces by The Signmaker, a ruthless enemy who somehow seemed to be able to be everywhere at once.

Yasmin wiped away tears. JJ snuffled.

'Why would anyone want him dead?' Captain Hunt asked.

'I...' Yasmin started.

'We have no idea,' Zander said.

The DARE winners traded knowing glances. They couldn't trust anyone, even if the pilot had just saved their lives.

'Hey, you're bleeding,' Captain Hunt said.

Ashen-faced, hands shaking, Zander glanced at the blood on his shirt.

On shaky legs, the flight attendant was already out of her seat, grabbing a first-aid kit from a cupboard.

As she tended to Zander's wound with HealFast strips, Captain Hunt pressed the heels of his hands to his temples.

'Are *you* all right?' Yasmin asked softly.

He nodded. 'Just one of my headaches. They come and

go. Nothing for you guys to worry about. I'm just glad you're all OK.'

'Thank you,' Dylan said. 'For . . . what you did back there.'

Captain Hunt nodded. 'Military training—taking action becomes second nature,' he said. 'I'd better get back into the cockpit and report to Miss Chen.'

The DARE winners gathered in the InvisiLounge.

'Report to—' Yasmin started to say.

Dylan held up a finger for silence and pressed play on his phone so it blared out Avarava's *Avaworldsava*. They huddled together.

'Report to Miss Chen,' Yasmin whispered under the music. 'That's what Captain Hunt just said.'

Zander shrugged. 'I think he meant "report" as in "report we are OK".'

'Can we trust Captain Hunt?' Yasmin asked.

JJ tilted his head. 'He *did* just save our lives.'

'True,' said Zander, 'but I do not think we can trust anyone. We keep what we know to ourselves, OK? Look what happened to the professor.'

Yasmin wiped a tear from her cheek. 'We got him killed, didn't we? We brought him into this.'

'The professor wanted to help,' Dylan said. 'He knew it was dangerous. He's a . . . hero.'

'Hero?' Yasmin shot back. 'That'll be a big comfort to his family!'

The boys stared at her.

'Sorry,' she said.

Dylan put a comforting hand on her shoulder. 'Only one person's to blame for what happened—The Signmaker.'

Zander's phone burbled and he glanced at the caller ID.

'Miss Chen,' he whispered.

Dylan paused the Avarava song as Felix's assistant appeared in the HoloSpace.

'Captain Hunt just told me what happened,' Miss Chen said. 'Are you all OK?'

They nodded.

'Could it have been an accident?' Miss Chen asked. 'A faulty fuel tank?'

'Are you kidding?' Yasmin snapped. 'His car was blown sky high!'

'It is true,' Zander said. 'No way it was an accident.'

Miss Chen blinked rapidly. 'But who would want to hurt the professor?'

Zander looked from Dylan to JJ to Yasmin. He saw distrust in their eyes. They weren't about to tell Miss Chen anything.

'We only met him today,' Zander said. 'How would we know?'

Miss Chen nodded. 'Of course.' Her tablet pinged and her phone tinkled. Miss Chen's eyes flitted behind her SmartGlasses. 'I will liaise with the local police—and report this to Felix. As soon as I know more, I will call you back.'

With that, she was gone.

Dylan put the music back on and they huddled together.

'Wow,' he said, 'she's so . . . calm. Too calm.'

JJ grimaced. 'It's like she wasn't surprised or upset at all.'

Yasmin shivered. 'And just before she left the airport she said she had "business to take care of"!'

'Yup, and then—boom!' JJ said.

'So you think she . . . what? Called in an air strike?' Dylan whispered.

Zander shook his head. 'I do not think it was a missile.'

'Right,' said JJ. 'We would've seen it streaking in.'

'Then a space laser like Captain Hunt was worried about?' Dylan asked. 'They're invisible, right?'

'Maybe there was a bomb in the car,' Yasmin said. 'Or on the road.'

A chill blanketed them. It was as if the sub-zero air outside the SpaceSkimmer had found its way inside.

'We do not know Miss Chen is definitely involved,' Dylan said. 'Just that it looks suspicious. But what we know for sure is The Signmaker knew the professor was coming with us. So how did he or she find out?'

'Obviously, Miss Chen knew,' Yasmin said. 'She had to clear the professor's travel.'

'She probably told Felix,' Zander said.

'Captain Hunt, the flight attendant,' Yasmin added.

Dylan nodded. 'Whoever the professor might have told. He could've said something to friends, family, colleagues. Made a phone call, sent an email.'

'But the professor promised to keep it quiet,' Yasmin said.

'No offence,' Dylan said, 'but we agreed to keep this between us unless we all decided. You and Zander decided to tell him.'

Yasmin's jaw dropped. 'That's not fair!'

Zander cracked his knuckles. 'You are blaming us?'

Dylan had his hands up. 'No, I'm not. Chill, OK? What I'm saying is that people say they'll keep things a secret but change their minds because they're sure they can trust people.'

Yasmin sighed. Zander took Dylan's point with a curt nod.

'So,' JJ said, with a cautious glance at his tense friends, 'we're saying a handful of people could've known.'

'Yes,' Dylan said, 'but they could've told a handful who told a handful. That could multiply pretty fast.'

'We must call the others,' Yasmin said softly, 'and tell them what has happened to the professor.'

After Yasmin's call, Mila, Isabel and Andy weren't noticing Madrid's cold night air anymore.

'I feel so guilty,' Mila said finally, her eyes shiny.

Isabel tucked a pink strand of hair under her beanie. 'We can't blame ourselves.'

'Yeah,' Andy said. 'This is all on The Signmaker.'

'I know,' Mila said, wiping tears from her cheeks. 'But . . . the professor would be alive if it wasn't for us, yes?'

'From what we knew of him,' Isabel said, voice stern, 'he would want us to keep going. Right now that means finding the journalist who wrote the story about the library explosion. Do you need me to make that call?'

Mila shook her head, took a deep breath, put her phone on speaker and dialled the newspaper's office.

'*Madrid Sentinel* newsroom,' said a bored-sounding man.

'Yes, I am calling for the reporter who did a story about the Madrid library bombing?'

'You do know it's after midnight,' he said grumpily. 'Vera's not here now.'

'Vera?'

'Yeah,' the man yawned. 'Vera Varkuna. Call back tomorrow after midday.'

'But I need to talk to her now, yes? Urgently.'

'What's this about?'

'I can only speak with Vera, OK? You can give me her mobile number, perhaps?'

'I can't do that,' he said. 'I could send a message. Have her call you.'

Mila looked at Isabel and Andy. They nodded.

'My name is Mila Cortez,' she told the man and gave him her number. 'It's urgent.'

'You said that already,' the man sighed. 'I'll see what I can do.'

Mila hung up and flicked to the Games Thinker website.

05:40:00

'Less than six hours!' she said. 'Maybe we must knock on the angry detective's door again?'

Andy rolled his eyes. 'I think he might shoot first, answer questions later.'

Isabel clenched her teeth. 'This is so frustrating! What can we—'

They all jumped as Mila's phone rang.

She answered on speaker.

'Is this Mila Cortez?' a woman asked.

'Yes.'

'This is Vera Varkuna of the *Madrid Sentinel*.'

Mila nodded excitedly. 'Miss Varkuna, my friends and I, we need to talk to you about the Madrid library bombing.'

'Now, in the middle of the night?'

'It's important.'

'Well,' Vera said with a yawn, 'talk.'

'Not over the phone,' Mila said. 'Can we meet?'

'Mila Cortez?' Vera asked, now sounding properly awake. 'The same Mila Cortez who won the DARE Award?'

'Yes.'

'This suddenly got *very* interesting,' Vera said. 'I'm sensing there's a story here.'

Andy nodded that Mila should agree.

'Yes,' she said. 'An exclusive. But I need to see you.'

'OK,' Vera said. 'I can meet you at the library. Give me an hour to get there!'

'What do you make of this?' asked Zander. Music was still blaring through the InvisiLounge of the SpaceSkimmer. He, Dylan, JJ and Yasmin had been trying to work out the best way to approach Luca Gabardi, given they would be reaching his house in the dead of night. They were getting nowhere when Zander silenced them to show a text from Miss Chen.

> Have booked you
> Infinity Hotel Pisa

The discussion turned to her motives—and how much they could trust her, if at all, and how they had little choice but to rely on Felix's mysterious and chilly assistant. Their murmuring was interrupted by a dramatic throat-clearing.

Captain Hunt stood in the lounge doorway.

'I just want you to know,' the pilot said, 'whatever you guys are into, I'll do anything I can to help.'

Zander bristled. 'We are not "into" anything.'

Captain Hunt eyeballed him. 'I saw the professor blown to bits in front of my own eyes. Then y'all turn up that music so you can talk without me hearing.'

Zander went to protest, but the pilot held up a hand to show that he wasn't finished. 'I'm not asking any questions.

I just want you to know that if you need anything, I'm here, OK?'

The DARE winners looked at each other.

Zander nodded. 'Thank you. We will keep that in mind.'

'OK, then. Y'all need to go back to your seats in a minute because we're coming in to Pisa airport,' Captain Hunt said with a smile. 'And I'd better get back to the controls.'

The taxi from the airport took them past Pisa's most famous landmark, the Leaning Tower, standing at its famously askew angle against the night sky.

'What a stuff-up,' Dylan said with a tired laugh. 'I wonder how the builder explained that.'

JJ chuckled. 'Yup, he was probably all like, "Come on, it's *almost* straight!"'

The taxi driver navigated Pisa's narrow maze of streets and pulled up outside Luca Gabardi's house. The family residence was a narrow three-storey building. All of its windows were dark.

'One-thirty in the morning,' Zander said as the cab drove away and left them on the empty street. 'Seriously, is our plan just to knock on the door? I would not be surprised if Luca's parents call the police.'

Dylan gulped. JJ's frown made him look like he was having second thoughts about his plan.

'Look,' Yasmin said, pointing at a window on the top floor. 'That could be Luca's room.'

They saw what she meant: even from the street it was obvious the glass had been decorated with Avarava stickers.

'OK,' JJ said. 'Leave this to me.'

'What are you going to do?' Dylan asked.

'Watch and learn,' JJ said, nodding at a park opposite the Gabardi house. 'You guys wait over there in the shadows. If anything goes wrong, there's no reason we should all get in trouble.'

Zander, Yasmin and Dylan hid in the bushes.

JJ crouched on the darkened street. He couldn't believe he was here, in Italy, about to try a Spiderman stunt. But he didn't have a choice. A ledge ran all the way around the building on the third floor. It didn't look very wide. But it would have to be wide enough. Concentrating, he cranked his robot legs up to maximum thrust. He'd never jumped this high before. Now was the time to set a personal best.

JJ sprang up off the road and soared into the night sky.

Then he was falling.

His arms shot out, hands grabbing on to the ledge.

Heart racing, JJ was hanging ten metres off the ground. If he dropped now, he wasn't sure if his robot legs would be enough to stop him from being horribly injured.

He heaved himself up onto the ledge. Glancing down over his shoulder, he saw Zander, Dylan and Yasmin's anxious faces staring up from the park.

Fingers gripping the gaps between bricks, feet gingerly stepping along the ledge, JJ edged across the front of the building until he reached the window with all the stickers.

He hoped that he wasn't about to wake up a parent or older sibling who just happened to love Avarava.

He peered into the bedroom. It was too dark to make anything or anyone out. JJ rapped his knuckles against the glass.

No response.

He knocked again, louder this time.

A bedside table light went on, and in the room a boy with tousled hair appeared from under the doona. The kid blinked, then his eyes went wide and his mouth dropped open when he saw JJ at his window.

Five minutes later, Luca Gabardi was saying quiet good-byes to JJ at the front door.

'That was amazing,' Yasmin said when JJ joined them in the park. Zander and Dylan nodded.

JJ grinned. 'I'm pretty sure Luca's going to wake up and think that was all a dream. But he told me what we need to know. He also gave me his word he'd keep my visit a secret.'

'So, spill!' Dylan urged.

'Luca's cousin shared a class with this strange kid. Parents work in London half the time and leave him to fend for himself even though he's only sixteen. Apparently a real programming genius. Anyway, he comes to school one day saying he's shortlisted for the DARE Awards.'

Dylan, Yasmin and Zander glanced at each other. The story sounded believable, because they had each received shortlist emails in the lead-up to being officially notified that they'd won.

'But when he didn't win, he said someone was gonna pay because he'd been unfairly accused of cheating on his application,' JJ said.

'Did you get his name?' Zander shifted restlessly.

JJ nodded. 'Rocco Aversa.'

A moment later, JJ had the address for the Aversa home. Dylan, Zander and Yasmin crowded around the phone screen.

'It's not far,' JJ said as he plotted a route on his map app. 'Ten-minute walk, tops.'

'Are we sure we should just confront him like this?' Yasmin asked. 'I mean, if he's The Signmaker . . .'

They were standing nervously at the end of the cobblestoned street that led to Rocco's house.

'What is he going to do?' Zander said.

'Well,' Dylan said with a nervous chuckle, 'there is the whole "killing us" thing.'

'He would have done that by now,' Zander said.

'Maybe he doesn't want to,' JJ said. 'But he will if he's cornered.'

Zander shrugged. 'Chances are this Rocco Aversa is just some big-mouthed kid with a serious case of sour grapes.'

JJ bit back his anger that Zander still wasn't taking this seriously. 'We're here,' he said curtly. 'So come on.'

They crept along the footpath between parked cars and shadowy townhouses. They stopped, just a few doors down from Rocco's place.

'Are you planning another one of your jumping stunts?' Zander asked JJ.

JJ sighed impatiently. 'I think we should take a more direct approach this time.'

Dylan frowned. 'You're just going to knock and say, "Excuse me and wakey-wakey, but are you The Signmaker?"'

He and Yasmin looked at each other uncertainly.

'Well?' Zander whispered.

'There's only four hours till the Third Sign,' JJ said. 'If that's what I have to do then—'

His eyes widened. The others whirled. A shadowy figure in a wide-brimmed hat and a long coat dashed from the Aversa townhouse, a bulging black backpack over one shoulder.

'Hey!' yelled Dylan, without thinking twice about the fact that the last time he'd taken on a bad guy, he'd copped a punch in the face. 'Stop!'

But the figure didn't—instead he wrenched open the driver's door of a BMW, threw his backpack into the car and jumped behind the steering wheel.

Dylan broke into a run. 'Stop!' he shouted. 'Hey, you s—'

Whatever he said next was drowned out as the BMW roared away from the kerb, tyres sending up a fog of smoke as they screeched on the cobblestones.

Dylan was left in its exhaust. Yasmin and Zander watched helplessly as the silver car sped away.

But JJ sprang into action. Robot legs blurring, he raced along the footpath in blistering pursuit.

The BMW was getting away, already halfway up the next block. But JJ didn't give up. He sped past a puttering Renault and overtook a buzzing Fiat.

Suddenly his way was blocked by a delivery van lurching from a side street. Moving too fast to stop, JJ yelled fiercely as he hurled himself high into the air and just cleared the vehicle's roof. JJ hit the road running, arms flailing to balance himself. He powered after the BMW, but the vehicle increased its lead.

JJ's SmartGlasses glimmered with an incoming call.

'Answer!' he yelled.

Zander's face appeared in the display.

'Bit busy right now,' JJ panted.

'I can help,' Zander said. 'Where are you?'

With the flick of an eye, JJ allowed his SmartGlasses to share his GPS coordinates. 'The BMW's a hundred metres ahead of me,' he said, 'and getting away.'

'OK, OK,' Zander said calmly. 'I have you mapped. The road curves up ahead. Next alley on your right. You can cut him off!'

JJ peeled off, darting into a dim laneway lined with smelly rubbish bins. Scrawny cats darted out of his way as his feet slapped against the cobblestones.

JJ burned out of the alley and shuddered to a stop on the side of the street. Only now did he wonder exactly what he was going to do when the BMW came roaring around the bend. If he stood in the middle of the road and tried to stop the car, it might just run him down. Even scarier was if the

BMW did slow down and he had to come face to face with Rocco Aversa.

JJ still hadn't moved when the delivery van approached. His heart sank when he saw it was being followed by the battered Fiat and then the Renault. 'No!' he said.

'What?' Zander asked in his SmartGlasses. 'What is happening?'

'The BMW,' JJ said. 'It's gone. I've lost it.'

'Oh,' Zander said, blinking in the display. 'How? There are no turn-offs!'

JJ's eyes went to the GPS map. Zander was right.

JJ looked down the street. For a few blocks, this part of Pisa was all apartment buildings.

'No!' JJ said again. 'He must've pulled into an underground car garage.'

Zander frowned. 'Any chance of finding him?'

JJ imagined the scenario. There could be a dozen or more car parks over multiple levels. Any could have rear exits into alleys like the one he'd run along.

'No chance,' he replied finally.

Zander nodded. 'Sorry for steering you wrong. Maybe if you had kept going you would have caught him.'

'Not your fault,' JJ said.

'Come back,' Zander said. 'He left the door open when he bolted. We are inside his house.'

As she followed Mila and Andy from the back seat of the car, Isabel let out an appreciative whistle at the National Library of Spain's floodlit arches and towering columns standing tall under the Spanish flag. Giant statues of famous Spaniards presided over wide marble stairs that led up from the street. But where one of them had been there was now a broken pedestal. The triple-seven graffiti had been scrubbed off, but the outline of the symbol was still visible. Mila took out her phone and snapped a close-up photo.

They fell silent as a green hybrid car purred to the side of the road outside the library. A round woman with auburn dreadlocks and a heavy knit dress worn with a denim jacket and boots climbed out of the car and trudged up the steps.

She broke into a wide smile as her eyes went from Mila to Isabel and then to Andy. 'Three DARE winners for the price of one,' she said. 'I guess this is my lucky night!'

They all shook Vera's hand.

'So . . . here we are—the scene of the crime,' the reporter said, 'with three DARE winners keen to see me about a bomb blast? There's got to be a story here. So, what's your interest in this?'

Andy leaned closer and turned on his brightest smile. 'Actually, as one journalist to another, is it all right if we keep this off the record just for the moment?'

Vera looked doubtful.

Andy put his hand over his heart. 'If you give me your number I promise we'll give you the exclusive once we know what's going on,' he said. 'But we can't do that until we know more.'

Vera frowned but nodded, handing Andy her business card.

'Thanks,' Andy said. 'We tried to talk to Detective Hugo Balboa but he was—'

'Angry and unhelpful?' said Vera.

Andy laughed. 'That's the guy!'

Vera grinned.

'We need to know if there was more information that's not in your story, yes?' Mila asked. 'We could not find any follow-up articles.'

'There's not much more to tell,' Vera said. 'Chemical testing revealed it was a homemade bomb using diethylbenzoate as a major ingredient, detonated with a trigger made from an ordinary mobile phone. But there were no suspects, no arrests, no real motive—officially, at least.'

'Officially?' Andy said, his journalistic senses tingling.

Vera pulled a tablet from her bag. They looked on as she played a video file. Grainy surveillance footage showed a figure in a hat and long coat with a backpack walking along the street and climbing the stairs.

Andy shuddered. The figure looked exactly like the person who'd ransacked Ryder's place and punched Dylan in the face! Same hat, same coat—he was sure of it! But he knew better than to say anything in front of Vera.

On the tablet's screen, the shadowy figure looked around before pulling a stencil and spray can from a coat pocket to quickly graffiti the symbol onto the pedestal. Then the person pulled a grey square of putty-looking material and set it up under the hem of the statue's robe before slinking down the stairs and disappearing along the street.

'That was four in the morning,' Vera said. Her finger fast-forwarded the video. 'Now, here it's thirty minutes later and—'

The image shuddered with a violent flash. When the smoke cleared, the statue had been reduced to rubble.

'The rest of it just shows the cops arriving,' Vera said, clicking off her tablet.

'Were there any ideas about what these . . . uh . . . arrows in the symbol mean?' asked Mila.

Vera shook her head. 'No. It didn't match up with any logos used by extremist political groups who're active in Spain or elsewhere in Europe.'

The DARE winners shared surreptitious glances. Clearly the reporter hadn't realised the arrows were actually sevens.

'Given there was only a destroyed statue and some weird graffiti tag,' Vera continued, 'Detective Balboa concluded that the bomber was probably just some crackpot.'

'You're not convinced?' Andy said.

'There were things that didn't make sense,' Vera said. 'I mean, who blows up a statue?'

'Sounds like you have a different idea?' Isabel asked.

'My theory is it went off accidentally and that the real target was the VIP who was due to visit the library later in the week.'

'Who was the VIP?' asked Isabel.

Vera frowned. 'Oh, come on, you know who.'

Andy shook his head. 'We really don't.'

The reporter looked from him to the girls and saw they had no idea what she was talking about. 'I thought that's why this was of interest to you.'

Andy's eyebrows shot up. 'Enlighten us.'

'The Madrid National Library was going to be the venue for one of those Digital Democracy debates,' Vera said.

Isabel nodded, but she saw Andy and Mila didn't know what Vera was talking about. 'I went to one as part of my Books not Guns campaign,' she told them. 'The Digital Democracy movement is about all people, rich and poor, getting equal access to the internet. It is very important, especially for education.'

'Yep, that's it,' said Vera. 'Well, the Madrid library DD event here was going to have Spanish computer experts, politicians and one very special surprise guest.'

Andy, Mila and Isabel were hanging on her every word.

'I learned that the special surprise guest,' Vera said, 'was going to be Felix Scott.'

'Quick, inside,' Dylan said, ushering JJ into the Aversa town-house and closing the door behind him. 'Are you all right?'

JJ tapped his legs. 'Yep, but after all tonight's excitement I might need an oil change earlier than expected.'

Dylan laughed. 'Come on.'

JJ followed him through a tasteful lounge room and up two flights of stairs to a teenage retreat overlooking the street. Yasmin turned from her watch at the window.

'JJ!' she whispered. 'That was so brave!'

Blushing, he looked around Rocco Aversa's large bedroom, which had its own bathroom. Under the yellow glow of ceiling downlights, it was a sweet set-up. He had a double bed, a lounge suite, a huge TV, a plush leather seat, a dedicated HoloSpace, gaming consoles, big bookshelves and a large wardrobe.

'Quite the lair,' Dylan said.

JJ nodded. But there were a few things that didn't look right. The bed was a tangled mess of sheets, there were pillows on the floor and a glass of milk had been left spilled on a rug. Near the lounge, a small coffee table was on its side and computer magazines were strewn across the floorboards.

'Is this what TV cops call "signs of a struggle"?' JJ asked.

Over in the room's office nook, Zander glanced up from

where a power charging station was conspicuously empty next to a desktop computer. 'Looks more to me like he cleared out in a hurry,' he said. 'Check it out—no phone, no laptop, no tablet. Just the work station here.'

'Reckon he had his computer gear in that backpack?' Dylan said.

Zander nodded from the desktop computer. 'Seems likely.'

JJ grinned. 'I guess you were wrong about this being a wild goose chase.'

'I owe you an apology,' Zander said, fingers flying over the keyboard. 'Innocent people do not tend to run like that.' He looked up gravely. 'Or wipe their hard drives.'

'But how did he know we were coming?' Dylan asked.

JJ shrugged. 'If he hacked our HoloSpace hook-up—'

Zander made a scoffing noise. 'I doubt he could beat my encryption app.'

'I said "if",' JJ countered. 'And *if* he did that, he could've seen us talking about Luca Gabardi and known we were going to investigate.'

'Except he had plenty of time to get away before we got here,' Yasmin pointed out.

'Maybe he only just found out,' Dylan interjected.

JJ frowned at him. 'What do you mean?'

He shrugged and pointed at the messy bed. 'The Signmaker has to sleep sometime, right? He can't be watching and listening in real time 24/7.'

Zander nodded. 'Good point. The other possibility is

that Rocco was tipped off.'

'By?' Dylan said, then his eyes lit up. 'Miss Chen?'

Zander shrugged. 'We cannot rule it out.'

'I guess this is Rocco,' Yasmin said, tapping a framed photo on the mantelpiece. Dylan stood by her. In the picture, Rocco Aversa sat at the computer where Zander now tapped away. He was solid and strong-looking, with broad shoulders, blond hair, cold blue eyes and a smirking smile. 'He gives me a bad feeling,' she said with a shudder as she used her phone to snap a picture of the photo.

Dylan rubbed his jaw, thinking back to that punch in Los Angeles. 'You can say that again.'

Zander let out a whistle.

'What have you got?' Yasmin asked.

'I can recover a few files. But they are encrypted.' Zander pulled a flash drive from his pocket and slotted it into the hard drive. 'Give me a minute.'

Behind them Dylan yelped. All eyes went to him as he backed away from the cupboard he'd just opened.

'What is it?' JJ asked.

Nestled amid board games was a mobile phone wired into grey putty.

'Is that a . . . bomb?' Yasmin gasped from the window.

'I think . . . yes,' Dylan whispered.

No-one dared move.

'We . . . have . . . to go,' hissed JJ.

'Wait!' Zander urged. 'What does the screen say?'

'Nothing,' Dylan replied. 'It's not on.'

'I think that means it is not armed.'

They all looked at Zander disbelievingly.

'You *think*?' JJ said.

Zander whirled. On the computer screen the file transfer bar was at eighty-two per cent and climbing steadily. 'I need another minute.'

Brakes screeched outside. Red and blue flashing lights filled the window.

'We haven't got a minute,' Yasmin hissed. 'A police car just pulled up outside.'

Beep-bip-beep.

All eyes went back to the cupboard. The phone's screen glowed with a countdown.

00:00:59
00:00:58

'It's armed!' JJ said. 'Get out of here!' He rushed for the door, Yasmin and Dylan right behind him.

'Come on, Zander!' Yasmin urged.

The file transfer bar had hit ninety-one per cent.

'I need more time!' he said, jumping up from the computer, ready to rip the USB free from its port.

Ninety-three per cent.

'Go! Go!' he said. 'I am right behind you!'

Yasmin froze behind JJ and Dylan at the bottom of the stairs. The shadows of police officers lurked behind the front door's frosted window panes.

'Mr Aversa,' a man's voice boomed. 'A neighbour reported a break-in! Are you all right in there?' The policeman banged loudly on the door. 'Open up!'

'Go,' Zander whispered as he came down the stairs. 'Backyard, quick!'

They rushed through the kitchen.

'There is a bomb!' Zander yelled at the police. 'Get away from the house!'

With urgent murmurs the shadows backed away from the door. Scrambling after the others, Zander heard the crackle of radios and calls for backup.

'Hurry!' Dylan said, standing by the open back gate.

Zander bolted into the alley that ran behind the house and he and the others surged along back fences, mentally counting down the seconds until—

'Get down!' JJ shouted.

They dived behind a dumpster.

Kerbamkaboosh!

The ground shook. Windows blew out. Car alarms wailed.

Peering up, the DARE winners saw Rocco's house was a blazing ruin belching smoke into Pisa's night sky.

'The house ... we ... oh,' Yasmin said shakily. 'We ... we were ... nearly—'

JJ tried to control his own trembling. 'Thank goodness we ... Is everyone OK?'

They nodded at each other.

'Come on,' Dylan said. 'There's going to be a million

more cops here in a minute.'

The DARE winners hurried to the end of the alley and forced themselves to walk away along the next street calmly. They zigzagged around corners and through streets until they arrived at a park outside a little church where they huddled, shielded from the street.

'So much for him not trying to kill us,' JJ whispered.

Zander shook his head. 'If he wanted us dead he would have blown the bomb as soon as we walked in. I think it was triggered because I got too close to whatever evidence was still on the computer.'

They looked at Zander.

'Please tell me you got it,' JJ said.

He held up his clenched fist and uncurled his fingers to show them that the flash drive was safely in his hand.

Sirens whooped nearby and a chopper clattered overhead, searchlight trained on the column of smoke rising into the sky.

'How do we get back to the hotel?' Yasmin whispered.

'No taxis,' Zander ordered. 'The police will monitor all vehicles coming in and out of this area.'

'Then what?' Dylan asked.

Zander's eyes flitted behind his SmartGlasses. 'It is four kilometres from here to the Infinity Hotel.'

'Walk?' Yasmin asked.

'If we stick to the shadows, we should be safe,' he said.

They were exhausted by the time they arrived at the hotel. After checking in, they set up in JJ's room. He, Yasmin and Dylan set up a HoloSpace with the others in Madrid while Zander bent over a desk, SmartGlasses hooked into a tablet as he tried to decrypt the flash drive. Bleary-eyed, and drinking coffees and colas to try to stay awake, the two groups shared what had happened and what they knew.

'We know Rocco's The Signmaker, right?' JJ said.

'Yes,' Dylan said emphatically. 'Unless the average Italian kids keeps bombs with his Scrabble set.' He shuddered. 'He was even dressed in the same weird outfit he had on at Ryder's apartment! What a psycho.'

'So,' Mila said, 'does this mean we say Felix and Miss Chen are *not* involved?'

'We can't rule anyone out,' Andy said.

Zander nodded. 'I agree.'

'Madrid library explosion,' Mila mused. 'The blast that kills the professor. The bomb that nearly kills you in Pisa. Explosions, they are The Signmaker's, what is the word ... ?'

'Trademark,' offered Isabel. 'But what I don't get is how he moves so fast. Rocco was in Alexandria to plant a bomb in the professor's car. But just hours later he's running out of his booby-trapped townhouse. What, does he have a SpaceSkimmer, too?'

JJ shook his head. 'Actually, he wouldn't need one. Pisa to Alexandria is only a couple of thousand kilometres. A private jet could fly it with plenty of time to spare.'

'All of this is very expensive, yes?' Mila asked.

'But anyone capable of pulling off The Signmaker's plan could've hacked *billions* of dollars,' Andy said.

JJ whistled. 'Or he might not be working alone. That sort of money would buy a lot of helpers.'

Dylan nodded. 'He could've paid someone to blow the professor up.'

The Games Thinker website hovered in the HoloSpace between them. The hours had escaped them and now only seconds remained. The tension increased.

'Can you unlock the files in time?' Isabel asked.

Zander looked up. His eyes were weary with defeat. 'I will need my home computers for this. Sorry.'

All eyes went to the Games Thinker countdown.

The DARE winners watched, pulses surging, fists clenched, mouths dry, eyes alert. Fear had woken them up.

$$00{:}00{:}03$$
$$00{:}00{:}02$$
$$00{:}00{:}01$$

Their phones vibrated and burbled with incoming messages.

The Games Thinker website's message changed.

STOP ME IF YOU CAN, DARE SEVEN.
12:56:59

'No more messing around with anagrams, then?' JJ said.

'Just symbols,' Andy said with a gulp. 'Open text message.' A shiver went through his soul at what appeared on his screen.

He flicked the death's head up into the HoloSpace. 'Skull and crossbones for me this time.'

 'I got it again, too,' Yasmin replied, sharing her symbol.

Her eyes were watery as she remembered how close she'd come to death after they'd received the Second Sign.

'It's OK, Yasmin,' Dylan said at her shoulder. 'We're all gonna have each other's backs, OK?'

She nodded.

Dylan added his symbol to the HoloSpace.

'It's just as the professor predicted,' he observed sadly. 'The symbol for Tuesday.'

 Mila flicked her symbol up. 'Mine is not anything I've ever seen before.'

Her friends couldn't identify it either.

'It points in four directions,' Zander said. 'Maybe a compass or something?'

'Could be.' Dylan shrugged. 'Isabel, what did you get?'

'Mine's ... creepy,' said Isabel.

'OK,' Andy said. 'People, tell me we're all seeing the same thing here? I'll go first. S-P-I-D-E-R spells spider.'

'Yes,' Zander said, unable to help grinning. 'It is what I see, too. Everyone?' There were nods all around.

'Spiders,' Mila said with a shudder. 'I hate them the worst. One great thing about Antarctica. No spiders, yes?'

'Mine's not quite as creepy-crawly,' JJ said, sharing his symbol in the HoloSpace.

'Circles and a cross,' Andy observed. 'They're so common. It could mean a lot of things.'

Zander added his symbol to the HoloSpace.

'Is that an owl?' Yasmin asked.

'Looks like it to me,' Andy said. 'A condor last time and an owl this time? Dylan, you're sure those anagrams didn't spell "The Birdwatcher"?'

No-one laughed.

The DARE winners lapsed into quiet contemplation of the seven symbols lined up in the HoloSpace between them.

'We've got the same problem as always,' JJ said. 'How do we know what order they go in?'

Mila shrugged. 'To have an idea, we need to talk interpretations, yes?'

'I'll make notes,' Isabel said. 'So let's do what the professor would have done by looking at these from every angle we can.'

'We'll get it this time,' Andy said.

'I wish the professor were here to help us,' Yasmin said with a sigh.

'But he is not,' Zander said. 'So we have to rely on ourselves, OK?'

She nodded.

'So,' JJ said, 'Dylan's is Tuesday?'

Everyone agreed. Mila did a quick search on symbols for Tuesday on her phone and flicked the results up into the HoloSpace. They matched.

'Tuesday,' she read, 'is named for Tyr, Norse god, also known as Mars, Roman god of war.'

'I've got an idea about these two,' Andy said, pointing at the skulls.

'Here we go,' Zander said with a roll of his eyes. 'Something about pirates, probably?'

Everyone laughed. Andy grinned. 'I'm serious this time, OK?'

He waited till he had their attention.

'Egypt was attacked and Yasmin got a skull in the Second Sign. Then the United States was hit and now we've both got skulls in the Third Sign.'

'What are you saying?' asked Zander.

'Maybe these aren't predicting anything,' Andy said. 'Maybe it's like fighter pilots painting their kills on the side of their planes? Two down. Five to go. It fits with the sevens, with Tuesday, with everything. I think The Signmaker is boasting to us that he has beaten us twice already, that people died and we couldn't stop it.'

The DARE winners traded glances.

'That's horrible,' Dylan said. 'But, yeah, I can see that.'

'OK,' Isabel said. 'Anyone else?'

When no-one spoke, JJ pointed at his symbol.

'Could it be X marks the spot like a treasure map?' JJ asked.

'Religions use the cross symbol,' said Andy.

'Chi,' Zander said, 'is symbolised by an X in the Greek alphabet.'

'Crosshairs?' said Dylan.

'What are crosshairs?' asked Mila.

'You know, like the telescopic sight on a rifle,' he said, miming shooting. 'It could be an assassination. Someone in the crosshairs.'

Andy gulped. 'Like Ryder was . . .'

A chill passed through them.

'That might fit with Vera's theory about Felix being the target of an assassination,' Zander said.

They looked at the X in the HoloSpace alongside the words 'Treasure', 'Religion', 'Chi', 'Map', 'Assassination'.

'OK, my one?' Mila said.

The DARE winners stared at it.

'Like I said, some sort of compass—east, west, north, south,' Zander offered.

'Quarter moons,' said Andy.

'Or shields,' said Dylan.

'With spears,' offered Zander.

'There is another cross in the middle,' added Isabel excitedly.

Mila pointed from her symbol to JJ's. 'Two crosses. Double cross. It means to betray, yes?'

'Smart,' said JJ, smiling at her.

'Any other suggestions?' Isabel asked.

They fell quiet, out of ideas.

The DARE winners gazed
at the spider.

'I still can't see how it's anything but a you-know-what,'
Andy said.

'Agreed,' Zander said. 'But what does a spider mean?'

Mila flinched. 'Apart from horrible?'

'Poisonous,' said Dylan. 'Australia's got plenty of
venomous spiders.'

Mila cleared her throat. 'A spider spins webs, so maybe
this symbol means the web as in the internet, yes?'

'A spider spins a web, a trap, and waits,' Yasmin said,
hugging herself. 'Are we the flies?'

A shiver went through them at the thought.

'OK,' said Andy. 'On to the owl.'

'In Egypt,' Yasmin continued, 'owls are the guardians of
the underworld.'

'Owls are associated with night,' JJ
mused. 'They can see in the dark.'

'Owls are supposed to be wise,' Dylan offered.

'They can rotate their heads, yes?' Mila said.

'Maybe it's saying we need to be wise and really look
around,' Isabel said.

'Owls say "who-who?",' Andy said.

Zander let out an exasperated sigh.

'I'm serious,' Andy protested. 'We have spent the past few days asking that very question: "Who?". I thought we were looking at every interpretation.'

They stared Isabel's notes in the HoloSpace.

Zander had a strange look in his eyes. Distant then panicked. 'Oh,' he whispered, 'oh, no.'

'Are you OK?' Yasmin asked.

He shook his head. 'I should have seen this straight away.'

'What?' she pressed.

With a gulp, Zander held up a coin he'd taken from his pocket. It was gold around the rim and silver at the centre.

'One euro,' he said in a shaky voice. 'The common European currency.'

He was met with frowns and nods.

'But,' Zander continued, 'each country has its own version.' He turned the coin to reveal an owl. 'This is the Greek euro showing Athena's owl.'

He held the coin beside the owl symbol in the HoloSpace.

The resemblance was uncanny. The DARE winners gasped.

Zander's expression darkened as he looked at each of them in turn. 'The next attack,' he said, voice dwindling before he composed himself and started over. 'The next attack is going to be on . . . Athens.'

The DARE winners felt the truth of his words hit them. The Greek capital as the target fitted perfectly with Dylan's theory that the attacks would hit their home cities. All eyes went to Zander. He gave them a look of steely determination.

'I have to call Captain Hunt,' he said. 'We need to get to the SpaceSkimmers and go to Athens. And I need to use my computers to find out what Rocco was trying to hide!'

Early morning Madrid traffic meant it took Andy, Isabel and Mila an hour to get to the SpaceSkimmer. Then it was another half an hour's flying time before Captain Demelo taxied the plane into the Infinity Air terminal in Athens. Since disembarking they had nervously paced the lounge waiting for Zander, Yasmin, Dylan and JJ to arrive. Zander had texted from the hotel in Pisa to say that they were having trouble finding Captain Hunt.

What they saw now on the room's big wall screens didn't set their minds at ease in the slightest.

The news headlines said the California death toll stood at two hundred and fifty. AutoDrive vehicles had been banned from the roads all across the United States. The news from Egypt wasn't any better. Cairo was at a standstill as soldiers took to the streets to try to maintain order. Further south, in poorer parts of Africa, panic was already gripping entire countries because aid supplies were going to be disrupted by the Suez Canal disaster. The three DARE winners listened fearfully as experts predicted starvation, disease and war across the continent.

Dipping his eyes to his phone provided no relief for Andy. The Games Thinker website ticked down relentlessly to the next event, which promised more destruction.

9:35:01

Finally, their four friends emerged from the Infinity air bridge.

'Dude, glad to see you!' Andy exclaimed, hand held up to Dylan for a high five. 'Up top!'

The Aussie smiled ear to ear and slapped his palm. 'Mate!'

They grabbed each other in a bear hug.

As Yasmin, Zander and JJ appeared, Isabel and Mila swept them into a big group embrace, watched by Captain Hunt.

'I see they found you at last,' called out Andy.

'He was enjoying his hotel breakfast, with his phone on silent,' growled Zander. 'So much for being there when we needed him.'

'I'm so glad you're all right,' Isabel said.

'Squeeze me any harder and I won't be!' JJ said with a laugh.

'It is so good to be together,' Yasmin said.

Andy and Dylan piled into the group for another round of hand-shaking, back-slapping and cheek-kissing. It was the first time all the DARE winners had been in the same place since New York. Even though these were extreme circumstances, it still felt like there was safety in numbers.

'Everyone, I think we should watch this,' said Mila, pointing to the news screens in the terminal lounge.

Behind a newsreader, the headline read,

PISA EXPLOSION: TEEN FEARED DEAD.

'Just after four this morning an explosion destroyed a town-house in Pisa,' a TV anchor was saying. 'It's feared that Rocco Aversa, sixteen, perished in the blast. Sources close to the investigation say police attended the scene after a neighbour reported a suspected break-in. Officers on the scene received a shouted warning from inside the house that there was a bomb. Seconds later the residence was destroyed in a fiery explosion that was heard twenty kilometres away and sent a plume of smoke high into the sky over Pisa. Rocco's parents, both working in London, are said to be in shock but are cooperating with police.'

'But we know he got out alive!' Yasmin said.

'Even if we almost didn't,' JJ added with a grimace.

Yasmin saw Zander on his haunches, his face buried in his hands.

Going over to him, she asked softly, 'Are you OK?'

He looked up and shook his head. 'No.'

'At least your grandfather's safe,' she offered.

'He is?' Andy asked. 'How's that?'

Zander straightened, recovering his composure. 'Before we left Pisa, I called and told him to take a ferry to an island resort off the Greek coast.'

'You didn't tell him why?' Andy said a bit too harshly.

'No,' Zander said. 'Just to trust me and leave. He should be safe.' He glanced at the Games Thinker countdown on his phone.

09:17:00

'We are wasting time! We need to get to my house so I can start decrypting this flash drive!'

'The Infinity Air steward said Miss Chen's got a big jeep waiting for us,' Isabel said.

The DARE winners looked at each other, all thinking the same thing: even though Rocco had been revealed as The Signmaker, they still harboured doubts about Miss Chen.

'Guys, we just stayed in hotels she booked and flew on planes she organised,' Yasmin said. 'I think we risk the jeep.'

Zander nodded. 'My scooter is still parked here. I will take that. Tell the driver to follow me.'

An Infinity Air attendant led them through the VIP customs area and ushered them out to the waiting jeep. As they piled into the vehicle's spacious passenger area, the jeep's powerful engine roared to life in response to the uniformed driver's fingerprint being recognised by the start button. An Infinity symbol appeared on the windshield, surrounding the words 'ID accepted' along with the driver's photo and licence number.

'Follow that bike,' Andy told the man as Zander roared off on his scooter. 'I've always wanted to say that.'

Isabel used a button on a console to slide up a privacy screen between them and the driver. She lined up the symbols in the HoloSpace.

'Zander, you cool if we work on these while we travel?' she said, linking him in. 'There's not a second to waste.'

'All good with me,' he said, face lit up by his helmet visor's video overlays.

'OK, then, let's go from most certain to least certain,' she said. 'Egypt was attacked. America was attacked. Next attack is on Tuesday—today—on Athens.'

'X marks some sort of spot,' Dylan continued. 'Or it could be a political assassination. Or there might be a double-cross involved.'

'Someone may be shot with a rifle or may be poisoned,' Yasmin added.

'But the spider could mean that the web is involved,' Mila said.

JJ sighed. 'Or we're walking into a trap.'

Andy looked around at the bewildered faces. 'There are too many angles.'

'He is right,' Zander said angrily. 'We have got too much to make any sense but not enough to warn anyone in Greece!'

The Signmaker

In the golden light of the HQ, The Signmaker felt a sense of satisfaction. Arrayed on the screens were scenes from California and Egypt. Death tolls and damages were still being calculated. But no-one could estimate what the long-term effects would be. No-one except The Signmaker.

Hard lessons were being learned in those places—and elsewhere around the world. Television and radio talkback, along with social media and internet forums, were filled with people asking not just what had happened but *who* was responsible and *why* these terrible events were happening.

Why: that was as important as *who*. Talk of computer glitches and catastrophic viruses and sophisticated hacks was a start. But the world would learn to look deeper than that. The world would need to look at itself to understand *why*. Then it would understand *who*. All in good time.

The Signmaker's plan was back on track. Things had been thrillingly close in Pisa. The DARE winners had come within seconds of thwarting the carefully laid plans. Yet The Signmaker had triumphed by turning a potential disaster into a promising deception. The web had been re-spun, and it was time to further ensnare the DARE winners. Now it was time to reach out to them and start a new phase of the game.

Now it was time to turn up the heat.

In the back of the jeep, Andy's phone burbled with an incoming text. The blood drained from his face.

'What does it say?' Yasmin asked.

With a swipe, Andy shared the message in the HoloSpace.

> Sorry to miss you in Pisa.
> See you very soon.

The jeep was filled with gasps. Dylan's eyes widened. Mila's hand shot to her mouth. JJ pressed his hands to his temples.

'Oh no,' Zander said from his scooter.

'It's from him?' Isabel said. 'From Rocco?'

Andy nodded. 'I think so.'

'"Miss you",' JJ repeated. 'As in, "didn't meet you" or "didn't kill you"?'

Yasmin shuddered.

'No, this could be ... good,' Andy said.

'What?' Mila asked. 'Good? You are crazy?'

Andy nodded. 'Contacting us like this? Acting all tough. We know his name. What he looks like. We're closing in on that sucker and he knows it!'

'Pah!' Isabel blurted. 'You think he's scared of us?'

'He should be,' Andy said. 'Because I'm gonna—'

'Shut up for a minute,' Zander ordered. 'Look! Out your left window!'

In the jeep, the DARE winners' eyes all went to a billboard standing over a petrol station. The advertisement featured portraits of four people below slogans written in Greek. There was a man with a big moustache, a silver-haired matron, a pudgy bald guy and a slender blonde woman with vivid green eyes. Despite their different appearances, they were all smiling, all giving the thumbs up, and all had their faces positioned next to circles with crosses in them!

'Just like my symbol!' said JJ.

'What is it? A political ad?' Dylan asked as the billboard slid past the jeep.

'Precisely,' Zander said. 'They are the leaders of the Work Education Business party.'

'Don't tell me there's an election today!' Andy said.

'No, it is next week.'

'But do you think it fits?' Yasmin asked.

'It may,' Zander replied. 'But the circled Xs are how Greeks vote using the online election system. Not that we need *more* angles. But Athens is the home of democracy.'

Isabel nodded and added 'Democracy' and 'Vote' to the symbol in the HoloSpace.

The Athenian suburbs melted away and suddenly they were on the coast, the motorway dipping to the Saronic Gulf, sparkling emerald and turquoise in the morning sun. Island shapes shimmered in the haze on the horizon.

The jeep tailed Zander's scooter as it whizzed through tunnels cut into the rock and past rocky beaches where grandmas in bathing caps splashed themselves in the calm waters.

Andy took it all in. 'Wow, this is awesome.'

'For sure,' Dylan replied. 'Great for snorkelling.'

They followed as Zander pulled off the road and up the driveway to a three-storey house with big balconies. After asking the driver to wait with the jeep, the DARE winners clambered from the vehicle and soaked up the view for a moment. Varkiza had beachfront resorts with thatch umbrellas facing a glorious expanse of blue ocean. All of this sun, sand and sea—accompanied by a gentle soundtrack of holidaymakers' laughter, rhythmic waves, the cry of seagulls and the purr of jet skis—made it hard to believe this very place might soon be under attack.

'This is so nice,' Yasmin said.

Zander nodded. But his expression remained serious.

'What is it?' she asked.

'My grandfather bought this house with insurance money after my parents died,' he said. 'To me it is always a reminder that they are ... gone.'

Dylan shook his head sadly. 'What happened?'

Isabel elbowed him in the ribs. 'Dylan!'

Zander sighed. 'It is OK. I want to remember them. They had a software business. But it was ruined by pirate companies. Copying their apps. Uploading them to the internet cheaply or for free. My parents did everything to save their life's work. Paid lawyers. Talked to the media. Worked around the clock. That is why they were in their office in Athens the night it caught fire.' He paused. 'I was thirteen.'

'I'm sorry,' Andy said. 'I have an idea of what it's like.'

Zander turned, jaw tense. 'You?'

'My mum died in an earthquake in Pakistan.'

'Oh, yes,' the Greek youth said, remembering that Andy dedicated his DARE Award to his mother. 'Sorry.'

'You never stop missing them,' Andy said gently.

Zander nodded. Andy gave him a reassuring smile. It seemed they might have finally stopped butting heads for a moment.

'Come on inside,' Zander said.

The DARE winners followed him along a garden path. He unlocked the front door and led them into a tiled foyer decorated with palms and statues.

'Welcome,' Zander said. 'No time to give you the grand tour. But does anyone want anything to eat? I know I am starving.'

'I could eat a horse and'—Andy yawned—'sleep for a week.'

Isabel caught his yawn. 'Any chance of coffee?'

'I will see what I can do,' Zander said.

'Need some help?' Yasmin asked.

He shook his head. 'You go upstairs. My bedroom is the second door on the left. That is where my computers are. I will be up in a second.'

The DARE winners glanced around Zander's bedroom. His bed was neatly made. The bookshelves were stacked with programming guides. Computer equipment was piled all over his long desk.

'Guys, look,' Mila said.

They followed her gaze to a side table with a framed photo of a younger Zander smiling with a man and woman. Their son had inherited their dark good looks. The DARE winners looked at each other sadly.

There was a rattle of china as Zander came into the bedroom with a big tray stacked with pastry triangles and lined with cups of coffee. He grabbed a pastry and a cup of coffee. 'Microwaved spanakopita and instant coffee,' he said. 'My grandfather would be ashamed. But it will keep us going. Help yourselves.'

The DARE winners were too hungry to be fussy. They descended on the tray, wolfing down the cheese and spinach triangles and adding milk and sugar to the bitter coffee.

'So, Rocco, what were you hiding?' Zander mused, sitting at his desk and slotting the flash drive into his computer.

The others crowded around his shoulders, munching and slurping loudly. Zander turned from his big screen. 'Guys, do not crowd me, OK? Sit anywhere. Just give me some space.'

The DARE winners spread out, taking spots on Zander's bed, on the couch by the window and on a beanbag on the floor.

'How long will the decrypting take?' Mila asked with a yawn.

Zander shrugged. 'Impossible to tell.' He sighed. 'It looks like I will have to run deep retrieval protocols first. Hours maybe.'

Andy looked at his phone. 'Just over eight hours on the Games Thinker website.'

'I know that!' Zander said. 'I will work as fast as I can.'

'I wasn't hassling!' Andy replied. 'I just meant the rest of us should use the time. See what else we can find to narrow down the symbols.'

Zander didn't respond, just tapped away at his keyboard as if he'd already forgotten the conversation and was lost in the numbers and letters scrolling down his screen.

Isabel spoke up. 'Why don't we each spend a few minutes seeing if we can come up with anything new from the symbols and my notes?'

They nodded, settled, and stared at their screens.

Tired eyes struggled to take in, or make any more sense of, the symbols. There were so many confusing and even contradictory meanings. It was hard to concentrate, especially as no-one had slept properly in days. Focus drifted, eyelids fluttered, heads nodded forward and, one by one, the DARE winners dozed off where they sat.

'Wake up!'

The angry voice snapped Andy into consciousness.

'Wake up, all of you!'

Andy blinked Zander's room into focus. Around him, Dylan and Mila and Isabel and JJ and Yasmin were looking sheepish as Zander paced the room like a caged tiger.

'You all fell asleep!' he seethed. 'I cannot believe this!'

'Zander,' Dylan said, getting off the couch, hands up in surrender. 'Sorry, mate—I just couldn't stay awake.'

'Me, too,' JJ confessed. 'I hadn't slept since . . . I don't know when.'

'Neither *have* I!' Zander said. 'But I did not fall asleep!'

'Sorry,' Isabel said, face red as she tamed her wayward pink hair with her headband.

'How long were we sleeping?' Mila asked

'It took me nearly four hours to decrypt the files!' Zander said.

'Four hours!' Yasmin's hand flew to her mouth.

Mila let out a yelp as she looked at the Games Thinker website on her phone.

04:19:12

Dylan gulped. Through the windows, the afternoon shadows were lengthening across Varkiza.

Zander shook his head in disgust. 'That was time I thought you were using to work on the symbols.'

Andy was on his feet, puffing up defensively. 'Wait, you didn't notice we were asleep?'

Zander stepped closer, eyes locked on Andy. 'You are *not* blaming this on me!'

Dylan got between them. 'Guys!'

Andy blinked. 'Sorry, Zander—it's on me, on us. We were so tired. We didn't do it on purpose.'

Around the room, the others were nodding.

Zander's fierce expression eased. 'For your information, I did not notice because when I am working I am totally in the zone. I do not notice *anything* around me.'

'We're really sorry,' Isabel said.

Zander nodded. 'All right, all right.'

'So,' JJ said, 'did you find anything?'

Zander returned to his computer. 'I was just about to have a look.'

Trading guilty glances, the other DARE winners gathered around him.

'Open,' he said.

Mila took a sharp breath, echoed by the gasps of others.

The folder contained files labelled with each of their names—along with others entitled 'Miss Chen', 'Ingredients', 'Infinity' and 'Log'.

Zander opened his own file first.

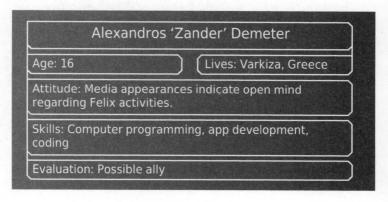

Alexandros 'Zander' Demeter

Age: 16

Lives: Varkiza, Greece

Attitude: Media appearances indicate open mind regarding Felix activities.

Skills: Computer programming, app development, coding

Evaluation: Possible ally

'Possible ally?' Zander said. 'Not a chance.'

'What's mine say?' Andy asked.

Zander brought it up.

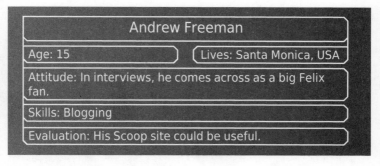

Andrew Freeman

Age: 15

Lives: Santa Monica, USA

Attitude: In interviews, he comes across as a big Felix fan.

Skills: Blogging

Evaluation: His Scoop site could be useful.

'Useful to discredit me with a hoax?' Andy said.

One by one, they read the files Rocco had compiled.

'"Parents could be useful",' Dylan read. 'Is that it? Yeah, thanks, Rocco.'

Isabel shuddered. '"Might be able to use her social media followers"! Ugh. What a creep.'

'Open file "Miss Chen",' Zander said.

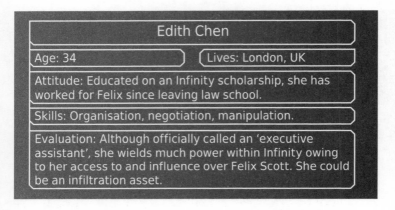

Edith Chen

Age: 34 | Lives: London, UK

Attitude: Educated on an Infinity scholarship, she has worked for Felix since leaving law school.

Skills: Organisation, negotiation, manipulation.

Evaluation: Although officially called an 'executive assistant', she wields much power within Infinity owing to her access to and influence over Felix Scott. She could be an infiltration asset.

'"Infiltration asset",' Mila read. 'What does that mean?'

Andy ran his fingers through his hair. 'This all sounds like Rocco was working out which of us he could use against Felix.'

Zander nodded and opened another file. 'Any of this mean anything to anyone?' he asked. 'Chemistry was never my best subject.'

Ingredients

Diethylbenzoate
Sulfhydryl acid
Monofluoride Hydrophosphate
Benzoic Pentamide

Mila's eyes were wide. 'Diethylbenzoate!' She said. 'Vera Varkuna said that was the chemical used to make the bomb in Madrid!'

'That's right,' Isabel agreed.

'But why's Rocco doing all of this?' said Andy. 'It can't

just be because he missed out on the DARE Awards.'

'This might explain it,' Zander said. He had opened the 'Infinity' file. It comprised scanned top-secret Infinity Corporation documents.

'Wow,' Andy said.

The DARE winners looked on in shock.

Corporate accountants warned that Infinity's debt could swamp the company. Infinity engineers feared the much-hyped flying cars would never be safe enough for mass production. Environmental reports criticised the impact Felix's South Pole resorts would have on the fragile ecosystem—and predicted they could worsen military tensions over Antarctic resources.

'Is Infinity really in that much trouble?' Yasmin asked softly.

'It doesn't look good,' Andy said. 'But these are alarm bells, not actual proof of any wrongdoing.'

'Uh, mate,' Dylan said, finger tracing rows of a spread-sheet that had come up. 'These look like "contributions" given to politicians for the "favours" they've done for Infinity Corporation. There are leaders here from countries all over the world.'

Andy squinted and then his face went ashen. 'Whoa.'

'Felix is corrupt?' Yasmin asked.

'You could interpret it that way,' Dylan said. 'I'm guessing Rocco has.'

'They are the only files I could retrieve,' said Zander. 'But I also managed to get this.'

He clicked on 'Log'. The screen filled with data strings and command codes.

```
D/:/[u]0001-geographiccache/creator/RA
D/:/[u]0002-banktransfers/creator/RA
D/:/[u]0003-videofiles/creator/RA
D/:/[u]0004-voiceprotocols/creator/RA
```

'What are these?' Isabel asked.

'Traces of folders that have been deleted,' Zander mused, eyes scanning the list. 'Look!'

He pointed to the middle of the screen.

```
D/:/[u]0014-directactions/creator/RA
D/:/[u]0015-symbolsresearch/creator/RA
D/:/[u]0016-enemieslist/creator/RA
D/:/[u]0017-accompliceorders/creator/RA
```

'Direct actions,' Yasmin read in a grave voice. 'Symbols, contacts, enemies list.'

'This is proof, yes?' Mila asked.

Zander nodded. 'I think this has to mean Rocco is The Signmaker. But what worries me most is "accomplice orders". That means he definitely is working with other people!'

Suddenly it seemed like there was no air in Zander's bedroom and that the walls were closing in a little. Everyone shifted, scared by what they'd just learned about their adversary—*adversaries*.

Isabel shuddered. 'I am trying to wrap my mind around this,' she said. 'So Rocco is furious that he misses out on the DARE Awards because he's falsely accused of cheating on his application?'

The others nodded for her to go on.

'So he's determined to have his revenge,' she continued. 'He hacks Infinity and finds out this bad stuff about Felix. He plans to blow Felix up in Madrid. And when that doesn't work he tries to frame him by unleashing attacks that end up benefiting Infinity to . . . what . . . turn people against Felix?'

Around her, the DARE winners raised eyebrows and shrugged shoulders.

'Yup,' JJ said. 'And by "yup" I mean "maybe" and by "maybe" I mean "I don't know".'

'It's a wild idea but I guess it fits?' Dylan offered.

Zander shook his head. 'It is one theory.'

'We need to keep open minds,' Andy agreed.

'Yes, why did Rocco not just go public with this information?' Yasmin said.

'No way he could've,' Andy said. 'This info was hacked. He got it illegally.'

'He could have leaked it,' Isabel said.

'Rich guys like Felix get away with things all the time,' Dylan countered. 'Leaking the information might not have led to anything.'

'But involving us, why?' Mila said.

'We got what he wanted—DARE Awards,' offered Yasmin. 'So maybe he is ruining our prize.' She let out a frustrated sigh. 'Maybe he is trying to show us he is smarter than we are. I do not know.'

'Killing hundreds of people for these reasons, it is insane, yes?' Mila said.

Zander frowned. 'Remember what the professor said: sometimes people believe such actions are justified to achieve their goals. I do not think it helps to simply think The Signmaker is crazy. There must be more to it. There must be a method to what we are calling "madness".'

'Still sounds totally cray-cray to me,' JJ said.

'Totally nuts,' Andy said. 'Sorry, Z-man.'

Zander went to argue but Isabel cut him off.

'So if Felix isn't The Signmaker,' she said, 'do we think we can go to him with what we know about Rocco and everything else?'

'How?' Zander shot back, pointing at the incriminating Infinity files. 'We suspect him of being corrupt. How can we trust him?'

Andy nodded. 'Hate to say it, but Zander's right. We don't know how Felix will react, what he might do to protect himself and Infinity.'

'Besides, we can't get to Felix without Miss Chen,' Dylan added with a shudder. 'Who knows if she was originally mentioned in the "accomplices" folder?'

A dread settled over the DARE winners. It was as if they were boxed in, trapped as much by what they knew as by what they didn't.

'So, what do we do?' JJ asked.

'What we need to do is find out what is about to happen in Greece!' Zander pushed himself up from the computer desk in frustration. 'There is nothing here that helps with that!'

'Breath of fresh air?' Andy suggested softly, nodding towards the balcony. 'Might do us good, help us clear our heads a bit?'

Below Zander's balcony, Varkiza's beach and town glowed in the afternoon sunshine. Seagulls cried, waves caressed the sand, and laughter and the tinkling music of an ice-cream truck floated on the salty air. But the DARE winners had no time to enjoy any of it. They huddled around a table with a HoloSpace between them.

'Does anyone have any new insights?' Isabel asked.

'I keep coming back to the ad for that political party,' said Zander. 'The cross used for voting in the election.'

'That might tie in with the idea of a rifle sight,' Dylan said. 'Political assassinations tend to ruin elections, right?'

'But my symbol?' Mila said. 'We need to know what it is!'

'The compass thingy,' said Andy. 'Oh, how I hate your stupid little beasts.'

'Beasts?' Zander said.

Andy looked a little embarrassed. 'My mind must have been working while I was asleep. Looking at it now I see creatures.' He pointed. 'See—legs, arms, heads, tails, and the square could be a body.'

'Yup,' JJ said. 'Lizards, maybe!' His eyes flitted behind his SmartGlasses. 'I'm searching for "two lizards".'

A moment later he shook his head. 'Nothing.'

'What about "two alligators"?' said Andy.

JJ did another search. 'Nothing.'

'I have a bingo!' said Mila, looking up from her phone, face flushed with excitement. 'I searched on "two croco-diles" and . . . look!'

With a swipe, she shared a website about African mythology.

Eyebrows shot up at what was now in the middle of the HoloSpace.

Mila's symbol!

'Crossed crocodiles represent democracy,' she read. 'Two creatures with one stomach symbolises the competing parties trying to win over the same population.'

Excitement rippled through them.

'Athens, democracy, assassination, election,' Isabel said. 'This has to be it! But who's the target?'

'Zander, the ad on the billboard,' Yasmin said. 'What did you say the name of the party was?'

He frowned. 'It translates as the "Work Education Business" party. That is what they are called in the English-language media.'

'Work. Education. Business,' Yasmin said. 'WEB.'

Zander nodded, eyes wide. 'Yes, that is the acronym people use!'

'Web!' Mila said. 'Like the spider!'

Zander quickly found the party's site.

'They say they are against the domination of work, education and business by multinational corporations,' he read. His eyes skimmed down the page. 'Look! They single out Infinity Corporation as being bad for Greece and bad for the world!'

'Could Rocco be going to kill one of the WEB party leaders and frame Felix for it?' Isabel asked.

'What are the WEB politicians doing today?' Andy asked impatiently.

'Hold on,' Zander said. 'I am looking.'

He scrolled through the party's news blog.

'They are campaigning,' he said, 'all over Athens. There are four of them. But . . . oh . . . oh . . .'

'What?' everyone demanded at once.

He looked up at them. 'Ariadne Mallas, their leader, is attending a debate tonight—at a Digital Democracy event that is part of the annual Athens Technopalooza!'

'Digital Democracy—Felix was going to one of those at the Madrid library!' Isabel added.

'What time is it on?' demanded Andy.

Zander's eyes frantically scanned the WEB site. 'Seven o'clock!'

'When the countdown runs out?' Yasmin said.

'Where is it happening?' Dylan asked.

'The Parthenon!' Zander said.

'That's that old ruin up on the hill, right?' Andy said.

Zander's expression darkened. 'The Parthenon is Greece's most famous building. It is *the* symbol of democracy. Killing a future leader there would be a disaster for my country.'

'This has to be it!' JJ said. 'Ariadne Mallas has to be the target, right?'

There were excited nods all around.

'Wait!' Isabel said.

She swiped a website into the HoloSpace.

TECHNOPALOOZA—ATHENS

Game launches include: Throne Raider, Mad Miles, Snappy Turtletime, Big Chef Party. App launches include: InfiniWeb Free Browser V2.0, StreamTime Deluxe, Eye2Eye.

'What is it?' Zander said impatiently.

'Don't you see?' she fired back. 'The bottom of the screen!'

Also: Digital Democracy debate between WEB party leader Ariadne Mallas and a Special Guest Speaker.

'Special guest speaker!' Andy said.

'You think it is Felix Scott, yes?' Mila asked.

'We already know he was supposed to do a Digital Democracy event in Madrid,' Isabel said.

JJ nodded. 'You think Rocco might still be going to kill him?'

'I don't know,' Isabel said. 'But we need to find out. I'm going to call Miss Chen.'

'What?' Andy blurted. 'You can't trust—'

'Trust *me*,' Isabel said. She put her finger to her lips as Miss Chen answered on speakerphone.

'Isabel,' she said. 'Is everything OK in Athens?'

'Everything is fine,' she replied.

'I have not found out anything more about the professor,' Miss Chen said. 'The Egyptian authorities are moving very slowly because of everything else they are dealing with.'

'I—we—appreciate you trying to find out,' Isabel said with genuine sadness. 'But the reason I'm calling is that Zander just told us about the Digital Democracy conference in Athens.'

The DARE winners eyeballed her, nervous about where she was going with this.

'We're all really interested in going,' Isabel continued. 'Can you arrange tickets?'

'Perfectly doable,' Miss Chen said, her choice of word sending a chill through the DARE winners. 'Infinity is launching our new InfiniWeb browser there, actually.'

'Is Felix the special guest speaker?' Isabel probed.

'Yes.'

'So we'll get to see him?'

'Yes,' Miss Chen said, 'but he will not get to see you.'

'What?'

'He agreed to do these Digital Democracy events by HoloSpace. He wants to be involved, but even with SpaceSkimmer speeds, the travel is just too tiring for him at the moment.'

Tiring. It wasn't a word they associated with Felix.

'Your Digital Democracy debate tickets will be waiting for you at the Acropolis gates,' Miss Chen said. 'Anything else?'

Isabel offered her thanks and hung up.

'Felix won't be there,' said Andy. 'So he *can't* be the target.'

'But does Rocco know that?' asked Zander. 'Your journalist friend Vera Varkuna apparently didn't know Felix was only going to be a virtual presence at the Madrid library.'

'If he's inside Infinity's systems,' JJ said, 'we have to assume he knows.'

'But this would mean Felix *wasn't* the target at the Madrid library?' Mila said, frowning. 'If the bomb wasn't meant for him, who was it meant for?'

The question hung there for a moment.

'We cannot worry about that now,' Zander said. 'We need to concentrate on saving Greece. If Felix is not going to be there tonight, it means Ariadne Mallas *is* the target.'

'If she gets shot it could look like Felix organised it,' Yasmin mused.

'Yup, like he literally silenced the opposition,' JJ added.

'After what happened last time, are we *sure* this is what the Third Sign means?' Isabel asked.

With a few finger swipes, Andy rearranged the symbols in the HoloSpace

'It all fits, doesn't it? On Tuesday in Athens the sniper rifle kills the figure at the centre of the WEB and destroys democracy!'

'We cannot let that happen!' Zander said, pacing the balcony.

'It says here,' Isabel said, looking up from her phone, 'Ariadne Mallas is tipped to be the next prime minister.'

Zander nodded. 'She is—and the murder of our country's most popular political leader would symbolise the death of democracy, which is what Greece prides itself on. We need to find her! Warn her!'

JJ nodded. 'Yup, then we go to the police and tell them what we know about Rocco Aversa?'

'Sounds like a plan,' Isabel said.

'How are we going to find her?' Andy asked.

Mila held out her phone. 'Does this help?'

The screen showed Ariadne Mallas's Twitter feed. The politician's most recent tweet was a selfie with a supporter. Columns of an ancient temple towered behind them.

'The Temple of Olympian Zeus!' Zander exclaimed.

'Where's that?' Andy said.

'Middle of Athens.'

'How long ago was that tweet?' Yasmin asked.

'One minute!' Mila said.

'There is no time to lose!' Zander said. 'Everyone into the jeep!'

The DARE winners hustled downstairs and piled into the back of the big car.

'Take us to the Temple of Olympian Zeus,' Zander said.

The driver turned the jeep onto the coast road. Isabel slid up the privacy screen.

'OK,' she said. 'Zander, are you OK to do the talking when we find Ariadne?'

He nodded.

Dylan frowned. 'Mate, what're you gonna say?'

'I do not think I should tell her everything,' Zander said.

Andy let out a cackle. 'Agreed—her first reaction would be that we're nuts!'

Ignoring him, Zander continued. 'I will just say that I—we—have credible evidence that there is going to be an assassination attempt.'

Isabel nodded. 'And ask her to do what?'

'I do not know. Delay the debate. See if—'

'Guys!' Mila said. 'I think we have the tail, yes?'

They saw the fear in her eyes and followed her nod to the back window.

A black sports car had overtaken a taxi and was pulling into the lane behind them. Its driver was only a shadow behind the tinted windshield.

The DARE winners stiffened.

Zander slid the privacy screen down. 'Driver,' he said. 'We think we have picked up a tail.'

'I see it,' the driver said, eyes steely in the rear-view mirror. 'Who is it?'

'Reporters,' Andy interjected smoothly. 'They can't get enough of us. Think you can shake them?'

The man grinned. 'Sure, as long as you pay the speeding fines,' he said.

'Let us worry about that,' Zander said. 'Just go!'

The driver stepped on the accelerator. The jeep sped towards the next cluster of vehicles ahead of them on the coast road.

Breathing hard, the DARE winners craned around to see how much distance they'd put between them and the sports car. Behind them their pursuer had also put the pedal to the metal. The dark, menacing car was keeping pace.

'He's still there!' JJ said.

'Don't worry,' the driver said. 'I have a plan.'

But the jeep was getting stuck behind cars. Traffic was pouring by on the other side of the road. The black car was closing in.

'Is it Rocco Aversa?' Yasmin whispered under the roar of the jeep's engine.

'Or one of his accomplices,' JJ said.

Terror struck the group. The other car might be packed with henchmen. They might have guns. They might be just trying to get close enough to shoot them!

'Guys,' JJ said, 'I think we should get down!'

The DARE winners flattened themselves as best they could in their seats.

'Hang on!' the driver yelled over his shoulder.

In a blare of horns, the jeep swerved onto the wrong side of the road.

Unable to help himself, Andy poked his head up.

The jeep had passed a sedan, and was racing by a station wagon. Through the windshield, a truck rushed towards them, headlights flashing, air horns blaring. They were seconds from a head-on. The jeep's engine roared as the driver strained to get by a panel van. Andy couldn't look. He ducked, bracing for impact, the others staring at him with wide eyes and pale faces.

The jeep veered suddenly. The DARE winners screamed, were thrown hard against each other and their seat belts as the driver swerved back onto the right side of the road.

'We're clear,' the driver said calmly.

Zander was first to sit up and look around. Through the back window he saw the station wagon, its driver waving his fist behind the windshield. But the sports car was nowhere to be seen, stuck behind the clump of cars and hemmed in by the oncoming traffic.

The other DARE winners sat up, breathing in short gasps, trading worried glances.

'That was insane,' Andy said to the driver, half admiring, half petrified.

The man shrugged. 'I know what I'm doing. Ten years with Athens highway patrol. Private driving pays better.'

They rounded a bend and came to a straight shot of road. The driver planted his foot on the accelerator to put serious distance between them and their pursuer.

'Can't see him back there,' he said when they were around the next curve. 'But as soon as we hit traffic he'll catch up. Let's be sure he's gone.'

With a smooth turn of the wheel, he steered the jeep onto a side road that led up a hill to a clump of trees that would hide them from view.

Bang!

In the back of the jeep, the DARE winners dived for cover.

Hearts racing, they looked at each other, expecting to see one of them had been shot. The jeep continued trundling up the road.

Whap-whap-whap.

'You OK back there?' the driver called.

Nervously, the DARE winners straightened up.

'We blew a tyre,' the driver said as he pulled into the cover of the trees. 'What did you think? That reporters are shooting at people now?'

The driver cut the ignition. The engine ticked as it cooled. A thrum rose from the road below them. Seconds later, the black car whizzed by and disappeared around the corner.

'See ya,' Andy said with a little salute. 'Wouldn't want to be ya.'

'Thanks,' Dylan said to the driver.

'All part of the service,' the man replied. 'But we aren't going anywhere until I change the tyre. Everyone out!'

The DARE winners stood in the shade of the trees as the driver worked the jack to raise the jeep. 'Rocco is the only one who would want to chase us like that, yes?' Mila asked quietly.

Isabel shrugged. 'Not necessarily. It's possible we were followed from Colombia.'

A chill ran through Dylan. 'Mate,' he said to Andy, 'the LA cops are gonna be after us about Ryder sooner or later, aren't they?'

Andy nodded.

Yasmin nodded, her expression dark. 'If Jackal had corrupt police friends they might come after me for revenge.'

JJ nervously patted his hair into place. 'My house was being watched by creepy dudes before I left Seoul.'

'Anyone watching you, Zander?' Andy asked.

Zander shot him a look and held up his phone showing the Games Thinker countdown.

```
02:45:22
```

'No,' he said. 'But I am watching time running out!'

An hour or so later, tyre fixed and with the driver flaunting the speed limit, the DARE winners hit the outskirts of Athens—and hit a wall of traffic.

'Sorry, but I can't do anything about this,' the driver said via intercom on the other side of his privacy screen.

'Could we run from here?' Yasmin whispered.

Zander checked his phone's GPS. They were still five kilometres from the Temple of Olympian Zeus. 'Is Ariadne still there?' he asked.

Mila looked up from her phone. 'She has not tweeted again. But a supporter posted a picture of her from three minutes ago. Hashtag said #Ariadne #OlympianZeus. We should still get to her in time.'

But time was running out for them to stop her assassination.

JJ glanced at the countdown.

01:46:35

Zander's dark eyes stared at the smoggy city streets. His fists were balled on his knees. Veins pulsed in his temples and his jaw was clenched. He looked wound so tight that he might shatter...

The DARE winners knew exactly how Zander felt

because they all felt the same way. The Signmaker—Rocco Aversa—had roped them into a terrible secret and it weighed heavily on them all. While the rest of the world reeled from disasters, only they knew that the worst was still to come.

'Should we try to call Ariadne?' Yasmin asked.

Zander shook his head. 'Even if we got through, she would probably think it was a hoax.'

Fifteen minutes later the jeep stopped at traffic lights beside a towering stone arch surrounded by camera-toting tourists.

'Hadrian's Gate,' Zander said, nodding at the colossal ruins peeking from above the tree-lined fence behind it. 'The Temple of Olympian Zeus is in there. Driver, we will get out here.'

'No,' Mila shouted as they reached for their doorhandles. All eyes went to her. 'Ariadne—she's at the Agora!'

She showed them the politician's Twitter feed with the hashtags #WEB #Meet&Greet #DigitalDemocracy.

'How long ago?' Zander said.

'Just posted,' Mila said.

'Driver,' Zander said, 'change of plan—can we get to the Agora?'

'Sure,' he said. 'I'll get us as close as I can. But it's pretty busy there with all the Technopalooza geeks there today.'

'Sorry to be dumb,' Dylan said. 'But what *is* the Agora?'

'A long time ago it was the centre of Athens,' Zander replied. 'It is a huge area full of old statues, temples and ruins. It is so massive that I am really not sure how we are going to find her.'

'We might be able to pinpoint Ariadne's location with these,' JJ offered, flicking up a Twitter feed based on *#Meet&Greet*. There were a dozen photos of people with Ariadne Mallas, all posted just in the past few minutes.

'Recognise any of those backdrops?' JJ asked.

Zander peered at them, shaking his head. Most of the pictures were close-ups of Ariadne with her smiling supporters.

The DARE winners watched the Twitter feed as the jeep weaved through the narrow streets. More photos popped up but still none offered any clue as to where Ariadne was.

The driver pulled the jeep up in a cobblestoned street flanked on one side by parkland and on the other by the steep slope of the Acropolis.

'This is as far as I can go,' he said.

A new photo appeared on the Twitter feed. Taken just seconds ago, this one was of Ariadne Mallas standing with a group of kids in front of a beautiful white temple.

'Is that the Acropolis?' Mila asked excitedly.

Zander shook his head. 'No! It is the Temple of Hephaestus! But it is not far!'

The DARE winners sprinted down the cobblestones of Apostolou Pavlou. The boulevard heaved with tourists feeding and watering themselves at cafes and restaurants. Hawkers shouted that they had water pistols, helium balloons, bang crackers and wind-up toys for sale cheap.

Over an ancient gate a flashing holograph proclaimed 'Agora Welcomes Technopalooza!'.

'This way!' Zander said, leading them through.

The others couldn't help but stop and stare. This event was amazing! Everywhere they looked the twisted trees and crumbling ruins had been transformed into a hub of buzzing kiosks crammed with the latest tech. Smiling geeks clutching show bags and wearing souvenir Technopalooza baseball caps oohed and aahed over curved screens, sleek consoles and the latest phones.

'Dude,' Andy panted, tugging Dylan's arm. 'Look!'

Posters for *Galactic Quest* featuring KitKat in heroic poses adorned a Virtual Reality tent where people acted out scenes from the films.

'Hi, Mum,' Dylan wheezed. 'Hi, Dad. Nice to see you. Call me sometime.'

Teenagers spun on gyroscopes covered with flashing lights. Colourful lasers criss-crossed the evening sky in amazing patterns. Giant floating HoloSpaces showed computer-generated life-size Spartans sword fighting with Persian warriors, in acknowledgment of the ancient location of the incredible modern display. All of it was set to a live rock soundtrack thumping from deeper inside the Agora.

Zander stopped and turned. 'Come on,' he shouted, exasperated, over the music and crowd buzz. 'There!'

Up ahead, the creamy columns of the Temple of Hephaestus rose up from a clearing. The DARE winners slowed, and crunched across the gravel. Clumps of tourists skirted the temple's low hedges as they took photos of the beautifully symmetrical monument.

Ariadne Mallas was nowhere to be seen.

'Hey,' Andy said, striding over to a plump guy with a goatee in a Yankees T-shirt. 'You American?'

The big guy nodded. 'Sure—from Louisiana. You?'

'LA,' Andy said.

'Ain't this great?' the man said. 'I'm here with—'

'Have you seen this woman?' Andy said, thrusting out his phone so he could see Ariadne Mallas's picture. 'Sorry, it's urgent.'

The guy pulled out his own phone and showed a selfie with Ariadne. 'Figured I should get a photo for the folks back home if she's famous. Locals were all excited and—'

'Which way did she go?' Zander demanded.

'Steady on, son,' the man said. 'No call for rudeness. Well, let me see, she said something about—'

'Agora Museum!' Mila yelled, looking up from her

phone. 'She just posted a photo about a press conference that's starting now!'

Zander whirled and pointed at a path that led deeper into the Agora. 'Quick!'

The DARE winners bolted after him—all except Andy, whose arm was being held tight by the American tourist.

'Dang!' the man said. 'I *do* know you. You won that Daring Prize, amirite?' Before Andy could react, the tourist was snapping selfies of them. 'Andy something, amirite?'

'Let me go!' Andy shouted, breaking free and running after the others.

'Hey,' the guy called after him, 'you're rude, too! I am so putting this up on ChatAbout!'

The DARE winners slowed at the steps to the Agora Museum. With its long portico and rows of columns, the graceful classical building had been constructed in the middle of the twentieth century in the exact style of the temple that had stood on the same spot two thousand years earlier.

'Whoa,' said Andy, eyes rising to the black glass and steel Agora Technology Tower that speared high into the night sky just beyond the museum.

'It is quite the contrast,' Zander said, to nods from the other DARE winners. 'It was built here to show how Greece has gone from the ancient to the modern.'

'Well, mission accomplished,' Andy observed. He looked at the Games Thinker website on his phone:

00:57:19

He nodded towards the Agora Museum.

'Come on!'

They walked briskly through room after room of price-less archaeological discoveries dating back thousands of years. There were glass displays of spears, pottery, jewellery, coins and lamps.

But in the room ahead there was a bottleneck of people, all crowding around a figure in the bright lights of news cameras. It had to be her: Ariadne Mallas!

The DARE winners got as close as they could.

Over the shoulders of admirers and onlookers, they could only catch glimpses of Ariadne. She was tall, dressed in a neat blue suit, with blonde hair to her shoulders.

'More than two thousand years ago, Athenians used the bronze tokens you see in these display cabinets to identify themselves as citizens so they could vote in elections,' she was saying to a reporter from an international TV network. 'Greece's history is the history of people power. It's right there in the word "democracy"—*demos* means "people", *kratia* means "rule". Tonight I will be debating a man who is so rich and powerful that he poses a threat to democracy, not just in Greece but in the whole world.'

'Is it Felix Scott?' the reporter asked. 'You've been very critical of him!'

Ariadne flashed a smile. 'It is,' she said. 'Felix Scott is known as the "Internet King", which means he is the most powerful person involved in what is the crucial technology of our time. The WEB party believes that it must be available to everyone equally everywhere, whether they are rich or poor. Tonight I look forward to asking Felix Scott if he is really committed to that goal. Without it, the world will never be truly free or fair. Given his power, Felix Scott needs to put people before profits.'

The room echoed with cheers and applause, and then the crowd followed Ariadne to the exit. As everyone spilled back into the courtyard, the gaggle of reporters, supporters and bystanders thinned.

'This is our chance,' Andy said.

Zander nodded.

Ariadne Mallas stood between columns posing for fan photos while two bodyguards waited a few metres away.

The DARE winners approached.

Ariadne's eyes widened when she saw them.

'Zander Demeter and the other DARE winners,' she said with a slightly patronising smile. 'To what do I owe the honour of a visit from Felix Scott's favourite young people?'

'Miss Mallas,' Zander said softly. 'Can we have a few moments of your time? In private?'

The politician's bodyguards glanced at their boss.

'I'm fine,' Ariadne said to her men. 'I haven't got much time before the debate. So, what is it?'

'It is a matter of life and death,' Zander said.

The politician's smile flatlined as she saw how serious the DARE winners were. 'Saying something like that is no joke—you need to explain yourself, and you've got one minute to do it.'

Taking a deep breath, Zander told her that while researching his latest app this afternoon he had stumbled across a chat room where suspicious coded talk made him curious. With the help of his friends, he had deciphered it and discovered that it was a plan to assassinate her at the Parthenon tonight. Andy couldn't help but be impressed at how believable he made the story sound.

'You must postpone,' Zander concluded. 'Felix Scott can do the same.'

Ariadne gazed at each of the DARE winners before her eyes came back to Zander. 'Let me get this straight: you're saying I'm going to be shot?'

'Some sort of assassination attempt is going to be made,' he said.

'Why didn't you call the police?'

Zander shifted from foot to foot. 'I—we—did not think they would believe us.'

Ariadne let out a long sigh and raked her fringe back from her forehead. 'I can't believe this.'

Zander nodded. 'It is a lot to take in.'

'Oh, you misunderstand me,' she said, voice rising. 'I mean I really *can't* believe that Felix Scott sent'—she looked at them all sadly—'*children* to try to scare me into backing down from the debate.'

'Hey, no, he didn't—' Andy said, stepping closer.

Suddenly a bodyguard was between him and Ariadne.

'Move back,' the man growled. 'Now.'

'If I'm not wrong,' Ariadne said as the other bodyguard got between her and the DARE winners, 'you and Dylan just perpetrated some kind of hoax on your website. So don't *you* tell *me* what's true.'

'Miss Mallas!' Mila said. 'You've got this—'

She silenced her with an upheld hand and looked at each of the DARE winners in turn. 'You all *do* realise you've just made a death threat against me?'

'We did not!' JJ objected.

'Did you or did you not say I'd be assassinated if I took the stage?' Ariadne said.

'We're trying to protect you,' Yasmin said angrily.

'You're *trying* my patience,' Ariadne snapped, looking at her bodyguards. 'Call this in to state security.'

A bodyguard whipped out a two-way radio.

'Now, wait a minute!' Zander said.

'We've got seven teenagers here,' the man barked into his radio. 'They've made a threat against Miss Mallas.'

'All we said was . . .' Dylan stammered.

'Yeah,' the bodyguard said, 'we'll keep 'em here until you arrive.'

'No,' Zander said. 'We . . .'

'Dude!' Andy cried. 'Enough talk! Everyone! *Run!*'

The DARE winners bolted from the colonnade, leaping into the courtyard as a bodyguard scrambled after them.

'Hey, stop!' the man cried.

Instead, the DARE winners dodged into the procession of show-bag-carrying tech geeks, hoping the thick crowds would hide them.

'Split up!' yelled Andy.

He glimpsed his friends peeling off onto the Agora's many paths. Andy sneaked behind a tent then dropped down into an ancient stone drain lined with weeds. He crouched in its shadows and started to duck walk across the Agora unseen, the sky above him criss-crossed with a new colourful laser show that had the crowds cheering. He hoped that thousands of people all staring up at the pretty lights would make it harder for the bodyguards and any state security to get through the crowds as they searched for him and his friends.

When Andy emerged from the drain near an exit gate, he hid behind a stand of poplars. Risking a look out, he saw the bodyguard pant into view. The man squinted around the shadows and palmed sweat from his brow. He shook his head to himself.

'Tell Miss Mallas I'm sorry,' he said into his radio. 'But they've all given me the slip!'

Andy's heart surged. His friends were all free!

A squelch of static came back at the bodyguard.

'Copy that,' his partner crackled over the radio. 'The state security guys say leave it to them. We've got to get Miss Mallas to the debate.'

Andy waited till the bodyguard went back the way he'd come. He took out his phone and texted the others:

> Bodyguards no longer chasing.
> Meet at Techno Tower?

Andy's pounding heart slowed as, one by one, his friends responded.

Andy stuck to the crowds and kept his eyes down as he made his way back across the Agora to the big courtyard that fronted the Technology Tower.

He couldn't help but grin as he spotted his friends arrayed casually on a bench, all wearing Technopalooza baseball caps pulled low and busy pretending to read games magazines from show bags.

Andy joined them. Dylan handed him a cap and he tugged it on. Now at least they looked like any of the other thousands of people thronging the area.

'That was a disaster,' Zander whispered. 'A total disaster.'

'Do you think the cops are really after us now?' Yasmin asked.

Andy nodded. 'I heard Ariadne's bodyguards saying state security were handling it.'

'By "it" they mean "us", yes?' Mila said with a gulp.

'But we're innocent!' Yasmin said.

'We didn't threaten Ariadne,' Isabel said angrily.

'A warning is not a threat,' Dylan protested.

'It's not,' Andy said, checking the Games Thinker website on his phone. 'But that might be the least of our worries in just over half an hour from now.'

00:36:32

'What are we going to do?' JJ said.

Zander got up from his bench and paced anxiously.

'Maybe she'll get nervous and cancel,' Yasmin offered.

Zander shook his head. 'She does not strike me as the nervous type.'

'I say we get our tickets,' Andy said, 'get to the Parthenon and do whatever we can to stop the debate.'

'Like what?' Zander said.

'I don't know—create some sort of scene,' Andy said.

'If we weren't already wanted by the police,' JJ said with a loud swallow, 'then that's a sure way to get ourselves arrested.'

'And,' Dylan said, sounding every bit as nervous, 'who's to say that Rocco won't start shooting anyway—and at us as well?'

Zander glanced at his phone.

'Time is running out!' he said. 'We have to—'

He stopped pacing, looking as if he was paralysed with fear.

'We have to try,' Andy finished for him. 'It's a risk we have to take.'

Zander was still standing frozen, staring at his phone.

'What?' Yasmin said. 'What is it?'

'This,' he said. 'Look!'

They crowded around him.

The Games Thinker site ticked away relentlessly.

00:35:54

'I know,' Andy said softly. 'That's why we have to go.'

'Not the time!' Zander said, his finger going to the symbol he needed to touch to close the website.

'The X in the circle,' he said. 'None of us considered it!'

The DARE winners gasped. Zander was right! All day, every day, that symbol was on every screen everywhere in the world.

Right in front of their eyes!

'It means to shut down, to close,' Isabel whispered.

'Also to delete,' said Mila.

Isabel flicked the symbols up into a little HoloSpace.

'Does it mean an assassination of a democratic leader?' she asked. 'Or maybe it's democracy that's going to be deleted?'

'How can you delete democracy?' Dylan said. 'It's a concept.'

Zander frowned. 'Greek elections are electronic. Delete that system and there is no election and no democracy.'

'That doesn't sound big enough for The Signmaker,' Andy said.

'Not big enough?' Zander snapped. 'Ruin the election and it symbolises destroying one of humanity's greatest achievements!'

'OK, OK,' Andy said, hands up in surrender. 'So, where's the election controlled from?'

They all looked at Zander.

His face was turned up to the black glass tower soaring above them, gleaming and reflecting the Agora's lasers and the Athens city lights.

'You are looking at it,' he said. 'All of Greece's crucial data is in the Technology Tower.'

'Is the election system connected to the internet?' Dylan asked. 'I mean, is it accessible?'

Zander frowned. 'Yeah. But they have assured everyone it is unhackable. Otherwise no-one would trust casting electronic votes.'

'Then to destroy the election system,' JJ said, 'wouldn't someone actually have to be inside the building?'

They stared at the tower.

'I think so,' Zander said.

'Rocco, he is in there?' Mila asked.

'Or is he hiding somewhere about to shoot Ariadne?' Andy asked.

Isabel's eyes went to the Games Thinker website on her phone.

00:31:19

'We have to decide!'

'I say we're being sidetracked by this "X",' Andy said. 'The Digital Democracy debate? Ariadne Mallas being a member of the WEB party? Felix being guest speaker? All of that *can't* be a coincidence. An assassination fits The Signmaker better than ruining some election that's a week away.'

Zander shook his head. 'We cannot ignore this!'

'We split up, try to cover both possibilities,' Dylan replied. 'Me, Zander and Mila go into the Technology Tower and raise the alarm. You guys go to the Parthenon and try to stop the debate.'

Zander nodded. 'It is the only way.'

The Technology Tower usually only served Greece's information and data needs, but to celebrate Technopalooza its huge lobby had been given over to interactive galleries and cutting-edge gadget displays. Frustratingly, this meant the Tower's glass revolving doors spun with a steady stream of tech geeks thrilled to get a rare glimpse inside the country's most famous new building.

Precious minutes ticked past as Zander, Dylan and Mila joined the throng queuing for a door.

'So, what's *our* plan?' Dylan asked nervously. 'Join a tour, find the mainframe room, hang from the ceiling on bungee cords and disarm the central computer?'

'You watch too many movies,' Zander said. 'We go inside. I introduce myself. Ask to speak to the Security Chief. Say there is a credible threat to the data. Tell them they have to be on guard against an intruder.'

'Yeah,' Dylan said with a grin, 'that worked so well with Ariadne.'

'Do you have a better idea?' Zander shot back.

'Boys!' Mila cut in. 'There's no time for fights, yes?'

Zander leading, they strode purposefully to the information desk.

'Can I help you?' the young receptionist asked.

'Who is your head of security?' Zander asked.

'Anthony Sarafina,' she said. 'Is there a problem?'

'Can you get him on the line and tell him Zander Demeter needs to see him?'

She frowned. 'Zander Demeter?' Suddenly the young woman's eyebrows shot up and she broke into a warm smile. 'You won the DARE Award! Sorry, I didn't recognise you straightaway!'

'That is OK,' Zander said. 'My friends and I, we need to see Mr Sarafina immediately. We have information that is vital to the security of this building.'

The young woman nodded. 'Of course, of course. Just let me call him.'

They stepped back as she dialled the Security Chief, explained what she'd been told, nodded and hung up. The receptionist waved them forward, brandishing three security passes.

'Take the first elevator,' she said, pointing to a bank of shiny lift doors on the far side of the floor. 'Mr Sarafina will meet you on the tenth floor.'

As they waited for the elevator, Mila gave her phone a quick look.

00:21:31

'Come on,' Dylan said, as the floor indicator counted down.

9 . . . 8 . . . 7 . . . 6 . . .

Zander stiffened beside him. 'Oh, no!'

'What?' Dylan asked.

Zander pointed at the far elevator, whose doors were just closing.

'Look!'

Dylan and Mila whirled. They glimpsed the figure. Wide hat. Face in shadow. Long coat. Black backpack. Then the elevator doors shut.

'Rocco!' Dylan gasped.

They rushed to the other elevator and watched the display to see where it stopped.

It paused at level ten . . . then sped upwards past three dozen more floors before stopping at R.

'Rooftop!' they said at once.

'What can he do up there?' Mila asked.

'Maybe he's going to climb down the side to the computer room!' Dylan said. 'Or . . .'

'Shoot Ariadne?' Mila finished.

Zander swallowed hard. 'It would be the perfect place to do it from!'

'We need to get up there!' Dylan said.

They hustled back to their elevator and piled in.

Zander stabbed his finger at the R for rooftop button.

The doors closed but the elevator didn't move.

Zander waved his security pass and tried the button again.

Nothing happened.

'The passes are only good for the tenth floor!' he said.

'We can tell Anthony Sarafina to get his security team

up to the rooftop!' Dylan said.

'What if he does not believe us, or we are too late?' Zander shot back.

'It's the only play we've got!' Dylan said.

Zander whipped out a keyring and used his scooter key to prise open the elevator's control box.

'You are kidding, yes?' Mila said. 'If you break those controls and we get stuck...'

He shook his head. 'These things are simple to override,' he said, quickly unplugging and reconnecting wires. 'Try it now.'

Mila hit the R button and it lit up. The elevator started ascending smoothly.

'That was amazing,' Dylan said.

Zander didn't smile. He just grimly watched the floors whizz by as the elevator took them to the top of the Technology Tower and to face The Signmaker.

The Parthenon was filled with WEB supporters. People stood shoulder to shoulder among the ruins, crowding around the temporary stage adorned with a podium, huge party banners and an Infinity Corporation logo that gave away the identity of the surprise guest.

Felix Scott was the name on everyone's lips—not that many in the crowd had much good to say about the man.

Keeping his cap pulled low, Andy hoped he wouldn't be recognised. He didn't think he'd be welcomed as a DARE winner by WEB supporters, much less by Ariadne's body-guards if they saw him among the crowd. He, JJ, Isabel and Yasmin had split up as soon as they were through the Parthenon's gates. Not only were they less likely to be recognised individually, but Andy reckoned his hastily conceived plan had a better chance of working if they were positioned in different parts of the crowd.

Shifting anxiously from foot to foot, Andy glanced at the Games Thinker site on his phone.

00:16:15

Andy shuddered as he turned in a circle. There had to be three thousand people here. Rocco Aversa could be anywhere in the crowd. But to get into the Parthenon, he would have had to pass through a metal detector. Maybe he had a plastic gun or ...

Andy whirled and looked at the Technology Tower. It was the only building with a commanding view of the Acropolis. From up there, an assassin with a rifle could easily pick off Ariadne. Andy's sweaty fingers went to the coil of little bang crackers he'd bought from one of the novelty sellers outside the Agora. JJ, Yasmin and Isabel all had strings of them, too.

When the Games Thinker website hit 00:10:00 they'd all ignite the little fireworks, whose packaging promised 'Big Bang Fun'. The plan was to set them off while they all simultaneously screamed, 'He's got a gun!' as loudly as possible.

Andy's hope was that there'd be enough panic and confusion that Ariadne's bodyguards would at least sweep her off stage as a precaution. Better she was the victim of a hoax than an assassination.

Andy worried about the plan working too well. Panicked people might stampede. The Parthenon's position atop the Acropolis meant there were plenty of low walls and deadly drops to the rocky slopes far below. He would never forgive himself if people fell to their deaths fleeing the fake gunshots they were going to create. Andy thought that Greek judges would never forgive him or the other DARE winners either.

'Desperate times,' he whispered to himself. 'Desperate measures.'

He realised that it was this sort of logic that The

Signmaker was using to justify his terrible actions.

'Ladies and gentlemen,' an amplified male voice said. 'Would you please welcome to the stage the leader of the WEB party and the next prime minister of Greece, Ariadne Mallas!'

The crowd roared as the politician approached the platform. But it was who she had just been talking to that made Andy's stomach turn inside out. There was no mistaking the woman standing to the side of the stage. Vera Varkuna! The *Madrid Sentinel* reporter. She'd followed them from Spain!

Dylan's heart rate soared as the elevator passed the tenth floor. Anthony Sarafina would be wondering what had happened to them. Maybe he'd identify them as a threat.

'What do we do when we get to the top?' Dylan asked.

Mila's eyes were wide. 'If Rocco has a gun, we are in trouble, yes?'

Zander nodded. 'We need the element of surprise.'

'Bit hard in a brightly lit elevator that's about to open!' Dylan said.

'The light!' Mila said. 'Smash it, yes? And be on the floor when the doors open!'

Zander nodded and jumped up, stabbing his scooter key at the fluoro strip. It popped, sprinkling a light rain of glass as the elevator was plunged into darkness.

The trio huddled on the floor, the only light now coming from the display showing the final floors passing by.

39 . . . 40 . . . *Ding!*

The doors slid open.

Dylan shut his eyes, bracing for a spray of gunfire that would end their lives.

All he heard was the wind.

He opened his eyes and saw the rooftop, silhouetted by the glow of Athens' city lights below and dotted with antennas and air-conditioning ducts. The whole expanse was enclosed by a security fence.

'Quick,' Zander hissed, using his backpack to prop open the doors and stop the elevator from returning to the lower floors. 'Out.'

Crouching, they crept into the centre of the roof.

'Is he here?' Mila whispered.

They couldn't see anyone in any direction.

Feeling more confident he wasn't about to be shot, Dylan hurried over to the security fence and examined its steel mesh.

'Intact,' he said, whirling round. 'Rocco didn't go over the side.'

'Look,' Mila whispered, 'down there.'

Below them, the Acropolis was lit up and they could see the crowd in the Parthenon. Somewhere, Andy and Yasmin and JJ and Isabel would be about to stage some sort of diversion.

'Where did he go?' Zander said, rattling the security grille on an air-conditioning duct. 'He can't have gone down there.'

'There!' cried Dylan, leading the others to the fire exit door on the far side of the roof.

Inside the stairwell, dim lighting showed concrete steps and railings spiralling down dizzily.

'He could be anywhere!' Mila said.

Dylan whipped out his phone.

00:14:33

'We have to find the Security Chief,' Dylan said. 'It's our only hope now!'

Zander nodded.

They sped from the stairwell and piled back into the darkened lift.

Zander grabbed his backpack and the doors slid closed. He punched the tenth-floor button and swiped the security card.

The elevator started to descend.

'What do we say?' Mila asked in the darkness.

'There is an intruder, and that he has to protect the election computer,' Zander said desperately. 'Anything! Anything to make him believe us!'

The elevator doors slid back at level ten. Zander used his backpack to block the doors again.

Anthony Sarafina wasn't waiting for them.

'Where is he?' Mila asked.

'This way,' Zander said, pointing at a sign with an arrow that read: *Office of the Security Chief.*

They ran the length of the corridor and paused outside Anthony Sarafina's door.

Zander knocked.

There was no response.

'We haven't got time for this!' Dylan said, twisting the handle and throwing open the door.

Mila screamed at what she saw.

Andy's heart pounded at the sight of Vera Varkuna lurking at the side of the Digital Democracy stage. How had she found them? How long had she been on their trail? Then a thought hit him. He whipped out his phone and texted the reporter.

You following us?
Black sports car?

Doing my job. Where R U?

This guy says you're
talking to Ariadne. Why?

It was a link to a selfie of the American tourist from the Temple of Hephaestus with Andy and the hashtags #DAREawards #DAREwinners #AndyFreeman #Badcelebrity.

Can't explain now

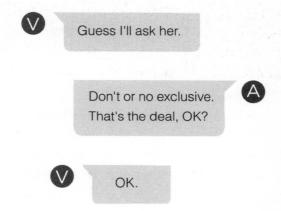

Breathing a sigh of relief, Andy tucked his phone away.

'Please also welcome,' the male voice was now saying, 'live from his supership the *Infinite Horizon*, Infinity Corporation founder and CEO, Mr Felix Scott!'

Felix appeared on stage as a life-size hologram, white hair shining and red suit vibrant.

'Greetings, Athens!' he said to a swell of begrudging claps and bad-tempered boos. 'Thanks for having me here at the Digital Democracy debate. I'm sorry I can't be there in person, but events of the past few days have made it impossible.'

Liar, Andy thought. *Miss Chen said you'd never planned to be here.*

But looking at Felix, he wondered whether the events of the past few days really had taken their toll. He looked old, tired, worn out, like his smile was pasted on.

'I'm glad to meet you, Mr Scott,' Ariadne said. 'And I look forward to a free and frank discussion. But before we begin,'

Ariadne went on, 'a funny thing happened on my way here tonight. It was something that really opened my eyes. I was approached by . . . well, let me say . . . friends of yours, Mr Scott.'

Andy's mind froze at what he was hearing.

Felix's grin seemed faker than ever. 'Oh, really? I have lots of friends, Miss Mallas. And lots of people who say they're my friends when they're anything but.'

Ariadne smiled. 'I'm sure you do. But these . . . friends . . . are quite well known. They told me that my life was in danger,' she said as the crowd murmured its disapproval. 'They tried to scare me into not talking to you!'

Andy's phone vibrated. He slipped it from his pocket.

 She's talking about you guys?

He swiped to the Games Thinker website.

00:13:52

Up on the stage, Felix was frowning. His holographic self had taken a step back from Ariadne, as if the accusation had physically pushed him.

'I can assure you I don't know what you're talking about,' he said.

As bad as Ariadne's public accusation was, Andy realised it'd help his plan. With her talking about death threats, the crowd would be primed to run scared when they heard what sounded like gunshots all around them.

'Such a threat,' Ariadne said now, 'just shows how scared big business is of the people power behind the WEB party!'

The crowd clapped and roared. Andy's heart felt like it was going to burst. With so much crowd noise the fire-crackers might not even be heard!

'Please,' Felix said, holding up his hands, 'I'm here to debate—not to answer unfounded allegations like this.'

The crowd burst into a new round of boos.

Ariadne silenced them with a raised hand.

'I was not—*am not*—going to be intimidated,' she said.

> **0:11:35**

Andy pulled the bang crackers from his pocket.

Suddenly they were flying from his grip as someone grabbed his arm and pulled him off balance. Andy lost his footing but was held up by strong hands gripping his biceps. Blinking, he saw he was face to face with two black-clad state security officers.

'Andrew Freeman,' said one cop. 'You're under arrest.'

'We'll take that,' his partner growled, pulling Andy's phone from his shirt pocket. 'You're coming with us.'

They started frogmarching him back down the Acropolis. Pinned between them, Andy could no longer see Ariadne or Felix. But he could still hear the politician making the most of the opportunity the DARE winners had inadvertently given her.

'...we won't be scared off, we won't back down...'

Despite his shock, Andy's mind counted off the remaining seconds as the cops hauled him down the path. When his friends threw their bang crackers, he'd use the moment to break free.

Three...

Two...

One...

Zero!

Nothing.

There were no loud bursts, nothing to send people into a panic, nothing to stop Ariadne and Felix's debate, or her assassination.

'What have you done with my friends?' he yelled at the cops. 'This is a mistake,' he told them angrily. 'The politician up there. She's in danger.'

'Sure she is—from creeps like you,' a cop said.

Andy kept struggling. Finally, as they approached a black police van, he spotted Yasmin and Isabel, both pinned like he was between cops.

Andy felt a surge of anger and frustration. But at least they didn't have JJ. Maybe he had seen them being caught and had been able to make his escape. Maybe he was safe. He hoped the same could be said for Ariadne just minutes from now.

'Get in,' a cop said. The three stepped up and plonked down on a bench as the officers slammed the metal doors.

'You guys sit tight,' a police voice said. 'We'll be back

with your other friends soon enough.'

They stomped away.

'Sorry,' Andy said, face miserable. 'I thought it was a good plan.'

'It was,' Yasmin offered. 'We just didn't get a chance to go through with it.'

Isabel nodded. 'A cop grabbed me almost as soon as I found a spot.'

'Me, too,' Yasmin said. 'I hope JJ got away.'

Andy pressed his face up to the barred plexiglas window. 'Ssh,' he said. 'Listen.'

Sitting in silence, they heard cheers carried to them from the Parthenon. Soon those sounds of celebration would turn to terror as an assassin's gunshots rang out.

Unless, Andy thought, *Zander was right.*

He hoped that he was. That the Third Sign hadn't been about Ariadne. That it had been about the election, and that Zander, Dylan and Mila had managed to save the Technology Tower computers from being compromised.

'How long until the countdown runs out?' Yasmin said.

'I don't know—they got my phone,' Andy said. 'I saw them throw it in the front of the van.'

Isabel nodded that theirs had been taken also. 'It can only be a couple of minutes.'

There was a commotion on the other side of the van doors.

'You've searched me,' a voice said. 'SmartGlasses are all I've got. Phones are for nerds!'

The doors opened and JJ stood there, dwarfed by the hulking cops.

'Get in,' an officer told him.

JJ nodded and hopped up.

'There's three more,' a cop said on the other side of the door. 'Let's go find 'em.'

As soon as the cops closed the doors, JJ grinned. 'I let them get me,' he said, pulling up his right jeans leg.

'What are you doing?' Yasmin asked.

JJ tapped the skin-coloured plastic of his robotic leg. A compartment opened. JJ reached into his leg. 'Useful to store your keys, wallet or'—he held up his phone—'this!'

'Quick, find out how long we've got!' Andy said.

A second later JJ had the Games Thinker website open.

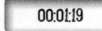

They gasped.

'We're out of time!' Yasmin said.

Andy nodded. 'Let's hope I was wrong and that the others have stopped The Signmaker.'

Mila gulped. 'We will know soon enough, yes?'

'Oh no!' Zander said.

A man in a grey suit lay in the centre of the room. His eyes stared sightlessly at the ceiling. Anthony Sarafina had a neat bullet hole in the middle of his forehead. Blood had formed a dark line down his temple and stained the carpet around his head.

Zander started towards the body but Dylan grabbed his arm. 'Don't!' he said, eyes going around the big office, landing on its heavy curtains, cupboards and closed doors leading to other rooms. 'Rocco might still be here,' he whispered. 'We need to go.'

Zander looked around wildly. 'We cannot. The computer room must be somewh—'

Brrraaaa-brrrraaaa-brrrrr-aaaa!

An ear-shattering alarm filled the air. A strip of red lights flashed along the ceiling.

'Security breach,' a calm robotic voice announced from a speaker by the door. 'Computer database compromised. Security Chief to report to level twelve secure control room to safeguard systems.'

But the only man who could do anything to save Greece now lay dead in front of them.

'We have to go!' Mila said.

'No!' Zander roared. 'We must get to level twelve! We

have to stop the attack!'

Dylan tore his phone from his pocket.

00:01:03

'We'll never make it!' he shouted. 'We have to go!' His panicked eyes went to the dead Security Chief. 'It's going to look like we killed him!' He wiped the doorhandle with his shirt front. 'Don't touch anything. We can't leave fingerprints!'

Zander nodded. 'Go!'

They bolted back to the elevator.

Zander scooped up his backpack as Mila stabbed at the G button with her elbow and then wiped down the rest of the panel with her sleeve.

The doors closed.

The elevator descended slowly. 4 . . . 3 . . . 2 . . .

They stood, trembling, fearful faces lit by Dylan's phone as the Games Thinker website countdown ran out.

00:00:02
00:00:01

They stared at the screen, unable to tear their eyes away. It flickered and the countdown reset.

Then the power in the lift went out.

'We have to get out of here.' Zander punched the door open button.

Nothing happened.

'Are we . . . trapped?' Dylan asked.

'Don't say that,' Mila said. 'Please.'

She looked as scared as Dylan felt. The space was so small, there couldn't be enough air to last them long. Who knew how long it might be before they were rescued? Who knew what was happening outside the elevator, outside the Technology Tower? Mila gripped his arm.

'Keep calm, you two,' Zander ordered. 'Help me try to open the doors!'

Dylan snapped out of his panic as Mila released his arm.

'Yeah, sure,' he said, setting his phone to flashlight and placing it on the floor.

Dylan and Mila hooked their fingers into the groove where the doors joined. Zander did the same. 'One, two, three!' he said.

'Uggggh!' Even the three of them, straining with all their might, couldn't open the elevator.

'Can you try to short-circuit it or something?' Dylan asked, trying to keep the desperation out of his voice.

Zander shook his head. 'Not without power.'

'The elevator stops at the moment the countdown reaches zero,' Mila said. 'This is not a coincidence.'

'It's not,' Dylan agreed.

'We should call the others, except—' Zander answered, frowning into his SmartGlasses.

'Except what?' Mila asked.

'My SmartGlasses do not work.' He pulled out his InfiniFone. 'Neither does this! My network is not just down. It says "No identity recognised for account".'

'What does that mean?' Dylan asked.

Zander frowned and shook his head that he didn't know.

'Mine still works!' Mila said, holding up her phone.

Dylan nodded. 'Same here! We can call the others. Get them to help us!'

He called Andy while Mila dialled Isabel.

Neither answered.

Neither did JJ.

Or Yasmin.

The texts they sent went unanswered.

'What's happening?' Mila said desperately.

'All I know is, we're trapped,' Dylan said, 'and as soon as someone finds us we'll be arrested for murdering the Security Chief!'

Ba-slam!

The van's doors flew open with the force of JJ's kick. The broken metal lock shattered across the cobblestones. Onlookers stared in shock as the DARE winners leaped from the vehicle and rushed around to its cabin.

'Hey, what're you doing?' a man asked.

'Saving the world!' Andy shouted.

At the front of the van, Isabel and Yasmin held JJ up off the ground. With another savage kick he smashed in the passenger-side window.

Isabel reached in, unlocked the door and scooped up their phones and SmartGlasses.

'Go!' Andy said.

Pedestrians scattered as they hammered up the street. Out of the corner of his eye, Andy saw Vera Varkuna, mouth agape, watching them make their escape.

'This way,' JJ said, leading them down a narrow street.

They pounded after him as he weaved up an alley that ran behind restaurants. A high stone wall topped with iron spikes blocked their way. Closed doors, big fences and stinking dumpsters hemmed them in on all sides.

'Dead end!' hissed Isabel, spinning round.

'Let's hide!' Andy said. 'Quick!' They squeezed behind a row of stinking dumpsters. Rats squeaked in the darkness and Yasmin squealed as she flicked a cockroach off her neck.

'Ssh!' Isabel hissed.

There was the *thwap-thwap* of boots on cobblestones down the alley.

They didn't dare breathe. Or move.

'That reporter said she saw them park their motor scooters at the end of this street,' said a cop. 'Come on!'

The cops hustled away.

Andy checked his phone then held it up for the others to see the message he'd received from Dylan.

> **D** Trapped in elevator.
> First floor. Tech Tower.
> In big trouble! Need help.

> **A** On our way!

Andy, JJ, Isabel and Yasmin ran back onto the boulevard and headed for the Agora's paths.

Even as they sprinted, worried sick about their friends, they realised that something was wrong. Very wrong. The Agora's tents were dark, the skies black and free of lasers. Everywhere, Greek people stared in confusion at dead phones and tablets and SmartGlasses.

It looked like Athens was blacked out. Or worse.

They slowed as they came out of the Agora and onto the road by the Technology Tower. Cars had stopped in the middle of the street. Puzzled people sat behind steering wheels, uselessly trying to restart their engines with fingerprint ID while other drivers leaned on their horns in frustration. Outside a restaurant, waiters brought candles to tables as diners prodded phones and tapped at SmartGlasses.

'It's not my fault!' a man was yelling at a waiter trying to swipe his credit card. 'There must be a glitch in the system.'

'What's happening?' Yasmin said.

'Nothing good,' Andy panted.

'Network outage?' asked Isabel.

'I think that's the best we can hope for,' said JJ. 'Look.'

Just a few feet away from the DARE winners a frustrated man banged on an ATM as people lined up behind him.

'It says none of my cards are valid!' he seethed. 'How can that be?'

'Get out of the way so I can use it!' the woman behind him yelled. As the DARE winners watched, she grew furious that the machine wasn't recognising her card either.

Across the road, hordes of people were stuck behind the glass doors of the darkened Technology Tower. Outside a man held his hand to the building's security scanner and shook his head.

'It's not recognising me!' he shouted.

Inside, a man crashed a fire extinguisher against a window.

Keeraaaash!

A sheet of plate glass shattered. Guards shouted for calm, but panicking people were already pouring through the window frame.

'Out of the way!' Andy yelled as he tried to push his way into the lobby.

'There!' Yasmin said, pointing to the fire stairs.

Andy led, followed by Isabel, Yasmin and JJ, pushing and yelling to get past the panicked visitors trying to get out the doors. It was like fighting a tide while climbing a mountain, with the surging crowd threatening to carry them back outside. But finally, they fought their way across the lobby to the stairs and raced up to the first floor, where the bank of elevators stood just next to the fire door.

'Guys!' Andy yelled.

'In here, mate!' came a muffled voice.

Andy, JJ, Isabel and Yasmin rushed to the doors.

'We'll try to pull them open,' Andy said. 'You try from your side.'

'Count of three,' Zander said. 'One, two, three!'

All seven DARE winners pulled—and the elevator doors inched open enough that they could see each other's fingers before they closed again.

'Hang on,' Isabel said, rushing to a glass cabinet on a wall that contained a fire axe. She returned and angled the steel blade where the doors joined. 'Try again and we can use this to prise it open.'

'One, two, three!' Yasmin said.

The DARE winners gave it their all, parting the doors enough for Isabel to wedge the axe into the gap.

'OK, we're gonna use the axe as a lever,' said Isabel. 'You guys push from your side.'

With much grunting and groaning, they inched the doors open. Mila squeezed into the corridor, followed by Dylan and then Zander. A minute later, they were downstairs and outside.

The DARE winners stuck to the shadows as people wandered the Technology Tower's courtyard in confusion.

'You were right,' Andy said to Zander. 'No-one shot at Ariadne. Sorry ... about everything.'

Zander looked stunned as he told them what had happened inside the tower. 'We thought he *was* going to shoot, from the roof. But it must have been to trick us so he could attack the computers.'

'But why murder the Security Chief?' Isabel asked.

Zander shook his head sadly. 'Rocco must have known he was the only one who had any hope of undoing the computer damage.'

'When they find the body, they're going to suspect we were involved,' Dylan said.

Mila nodded. 'We asked to see him and then ...'

Isabel tugged at her hair. 'And we just escaped custody.'

'What?' Dylan asked.

She explained how they'd been caught. 'If it hadn't been for JJ, we'd still be in the police van.'

'This means that we are all fugitives,' Yasmin said.

'And another thing,' Andy said. 'Vera Varkuna was back there. I saw her with Ariadne Mallas. She was the one in the black sports car!'

'What?' Isabel said.

He quickly explained their text exchanges.

'That's the reporter the cops mentioned?' JJ asked. 'The one who said we were on motor scooters?'

Andy nodded. 'She lied to them. She wants to protect her exclusive.'

'She's the least of our worries now,' Isabel said. 'What I want to know is why the power is all out, why everything has stopped working. The election system shouldn't have affected that?'

'I do not know,' Zander admitted, sitting heavily, head in hands. 'All I know is we failed . . . I failed.'

'We did everything we could!' Yasmin said.

Dylan crouched by him. 'Mate,' he said, 'you came so close. You can't blame yourself, all right. But right now we have to get out of the city, OK?'

Isabel leaned down. 'Dylan's right, Zander, the city's no place to be. Not if all the power's gone and people are freaking out. Not if the police are looking for us.'

'I think we need to get out of Greece,' Andy said. 'If we're to have any chance of saving the next place.'

Zander reared up. 'The next place?' he said angrily.

Andy held his ground. 'Sorry, but I'm right. We can't do anything here, can we?'

Zander gulped back a sob but nodded. 'Yeah. Yeah.'

'OK,' Isabel said softly, 'I'll call Captain Hunt.' While the others listened, she dialled the pilot. 'Hello, Captain Hunt.' She listened and nodded. 'We are. Can we fly out tonight?'

Isabel frowned. 'No. Yes. Oh, no. Yes, we're in downtown. No, the lights are out. Cars aren't working.' Isabel's eyes went wide. 'The whole country?' She listened. 'No, we're not hurt.' She shook her head at the others. 'OK. We'll call you back soon.' Isabel hung up.

'What is it?' Zander said, eyes wide, throat bobbing. 'Tell me.'

'Captain Hunt says it's all over the news,' Isabel said. 'Greece has been ... wiped out.'

Zanders face went slack with shock. 'Wiped out?' he said softly. 'What ... what?'

Yasmin put a comforting hand on his shoulder.

'What does that mean?' Andy finished for Zander.

'Captain Hunt,' Isabel continued reluctantly, 'said that all of Greece's data is just ... gone.'

'All of it?' Zander whispered.

Isabel nodded. 'Identities, government records, bank accounts and phone IDs, electricity and gas accounts—all of it.'

Zander put his head in his hands. 'That is why my phone and SmartGlasses do not work. Your comms can access your data from networks in other countries or satellites. Mine cannot because what my account is based on—my digital identity—is now ... *gone*.'

Isabel looked at the others, unsure whether or not to

keep going with the bad news. 'We can't fly out,' she said softly. 'Captain Hunt says all flights in and out have been suspended.'

JJ held up his phone, showing a breaking-news update.

'Greece has suffered what technology experts are calling Datageddon,' the anchor said. 'It appears that the entire nation's electronically stored information has been erased. All Greek mobile phones and internet services are useless. Streets and highways are jammed because cars no longer recognise their drivers' identities. Similarly, the erasure of staff IDs has shut down public transport along with air traffic control systems. Already we're hearing reports of panic across the country as people rush stores and use whatever cash they have to buy survival essentials.'

Zander let out a bitter laugh.

'What?' Yasmin asked softly.

'*Demos*—"the people",' he reminded them. 'You do not get it?'

The others shook their heads.

Zander blinked, dark eyes glittering with anger. 'We were focused on Ariadne, one person, one politician. But it's the *people* that are *the* most important part of the democracy. Citizenship depends on identity. Now . . . it is all gone. Everything that made Greece has been wiped out!'

Shouts reached the DARE winners from a restaurant where diners and waiters were clashing over unpaid bills. There was a flurry of fists and the *smack!* of a punch cracking a jaw. Two doors down, the glass window of a convenience store shattered and a man ran from the door bleeding from the head, his arms clutching loaves of bread and bottles of milk. Other shadowy figures bustled along the darkened street saying ugly things about bashing and smashing and grabbing.

Crack! Crack!

They all flinched, ducked, clung together in the shadows.

'Was that gunfire?' Andy said.

Isabel nodded. 'I'd know it anywhere.'

JJ showed them his phone.

'Downtown Athens is rapidly descending into chaos,' the news anchor said over video of cars burning outside the Greek Parliament. 'Reports say some police have joined looters and that violence is breaking out all across the city.'

'What are we going to do?' Yasmin said. 'Where do we go?'

'To the coast,' Zander said. 'If we can make it to a port, there will be boats from other countries that are still operational. Maybe we can get one out of Greece.'

'How far is it to the coast?' Dylan asked.

'Fifteen kilometres,' Zander said.

'How do we get there?' Mila asked.

'Walk, yeah?' Andy said.

Zander nodded.

'If we get trapped in Greece,' Mila said, 'we won't be able to do anything about the next sign, yes?'

Dylan nodded. 'Australia's going to be next'—he looked at JJ, Isabel and Mila—'or South Korea or Colombia or Antarctica. We need to be able to get to wherever we're needed.'

'This way,' Zander said, face lit up by the GPS on JJ's phone. 'Stay out of sight.'

Doubled over, he scurried along a dark alley, the DARE winners following.

They huddled by a derelict building and looked along Andrea Syngrou Avenue. What had just hours earlier been busy with traffic was now clogged with stopped cars and buses. Here and there, a few motorists were making slight progress by honking people out of the way on the footpaths.

'Why are some cars OK?' Yasmin asked.

'They look like older models,' JJ said. 'Started with old-fashioned keys rather than fingerprints, voice recognition or retina scans.'

But even those cars couldn't get far amid the stalled vehicles and chaos.

Looters carried televisions from one shattered store. More thieves were taking jewellery from another wrecked shopfront. Alarms rang everywhere.

'What are people doing?' Isabel said.

'Showing their true colours,' Zander said with disgust. 'Taking what they can get.'

He slipped his SmartGlasses on.

'Working?' Andy asked.

Zander's eyes flicked back and forward. He shook his head. 'It will not boot. Once I get out of Greece I might be able to reboot using a new ID.'

Andy's eyes went to a car burning out of control. 'Getting out of the country sounds good for a lot of reasons.'

Further up towards the city more fires were blazing unchecked. The air was filled with the *crack* of gunfire and explosions but only occasionally pierced by sirens.

'This place is turning into a war zone,' Andy said. 'Where are the emergency services?'

Zander shook his head. 'Firefighters, police, para-medics—they all have IDs to get into buildings, start vehicles and access communications.'

'So they're as helpless as everyone else?' Mila asked with a gulp.

He nodded sadly. 'Looks that way.'

Dylan peered at the GPS. 'Do we follow this road, Syngrou, to the coast?'

Zander shook his head. 'Too dangerous.'

Whhomppfa!

Out on the big avenue, a group of men laughed and danced around a newsstand they'd just set on fire. They shrieked as little explosions erupted around their feet and thick tear gas began to drift up before a trio of mask-wearing riot cops swept in with their batons swinging brutally.

Yasmin shuddered at the screams before the tear gas obscured their view of the violence. 'We have to get out of here!'

Zander nodded, staring at JJ's phone. His finger traced the maze of smaller streets that criss-crossed Athens to the coast. 'This way will be safer—I think.'

Feeling like rats who had to hug the darkness to survive, they streamed across a broad avenue, keeping their heads down as they scurried between cars.

A barrage of gunfire erupted.

Bullets *thunked* into cars and *pinged* off buildings as the DARE winners scrambled off the boulevard.

'Run!' Andy yelled. 'Don't stop!'

Blood surging, minds reeling, they ran deeper into the city that had broken down into a series of bloody running battles.

The Signmaker watched the DARE winners try to make their escape through the darkness of the Athenian maze. Seeing them band together like this, the mastermind continued to be impressed by their bravery and resourcefulness. Although there had been close calls, the plan had come together perfectly. The diversions had worked, physical access had been gained and another swarm of nanobots had been unleashed to knock out the Technology Tower's servers while the one human obstacle had been eliminated.

The DARE winners were more in the dark than ever. So was Greece. Just like the rest of the world, the home of philosophy and democracy had come to depend entirely on modern technology. The Wipeout had shown how fearful, ignorant and violent people were when that access was suddenly removed. Hundreds would likely perish in the anarchy of the coming hours and days, weeks and months.

The Signmaker's mind went to the next attack. What was coming would be bigger and more brutal than all that had come before. These attacks, the mastermind believed, were no different from a doctor vaccinating against deadly illnesses or a surgeon amputating terribly diseased limbs.

Painful. Tragic. Necessary.

Sometimes great suffering was needed to ensure survival.

For hours, the DARE winners crept along the streets, hurried past yards and sheltered beside cars. As they got farther from the centre of city, there were fewer people out and more fearful candlelit faces glimpsing through the windows of blacked-out houses. But even in the suburbs, the smoky air echoed with shouts, shots and screams.

'Guys,' Dylan said, shining his phone's flashlight on a gleaming water fountain in a little park, 'can we get a drink, have a bit of a rest?'

There were cautious nods from his friends. Eyes on the black fringe of shrubs, they edged into the park and took turns at the drinking fountain.

'That hits the spot,' JJ said, wiping water from his mouth with a grin. 'I'm thinking I don't need to rest my feet quite as much as you guys.'

Wearily, they arranged themselves on a wooden bench.

'How far now?' Yasmin asked.

Zander checked the GPS. 'Halfway there,' he said.

'Should we ask Miss Chen for an update?'

An hour ago, when they'd felt less threatened by the craziness erupting in the city, Zander had called Felix's assistant and forced himself to speak calmly as he asked her to get a boat to pick them up from the port at Piraeus. She had said she'd do what she could. Since then there had been no word.

'We should leave it a while longer,' he said.

Now that they were stopped, Mila glanced again at the Games Thinker website. 'Guys, look!' she cried, holding up her phone.

'What?!' Dylan exclaimed.

'What do we do?' Isabel wondered.

'There is no way to "choose carefully", is there?' Mila said. 'Seven doors. A one in seven chance to be right. But we do not even know what we are choosing, no?'

Isabel sighed. 'Whatever we guess, it's a six out of seven chance we'll get it wrong.'

'And what happens then?' Yasmin said. 'Maybe we, I don't know, blow up the world?'

Andy shook his head. 'That doesn't seem like it would fit with The Signmaker's plan, does it?'

'Can't we just leave it?' Isabel said. 'Until we know more?'

'That is the problem, yes?' Mila replied, pointing at the countdown. 'We are running out of time. If there's any clue behind these doors that can help us now, we should take the chance, yes? It might give us information we can work on while we keep walking.'

'Vote?' Andy said.

Zander raised his hand. 'I am for taking a chance.'

One by one, the others voted in favour, Isabel raising her hand last.

'OK,' Mila said. 'Now we just have to decide which door.'

'There's no way to know, is there?' Yasmin asked.

JJ shook his head. 'If I can make the obvious suggestion?'

They were all ears.

'The seventh door,' he said. 'Seven is the key to all of this, right?'

It made perfect sense.

'I'll do it,' he said, easing his fingertip towards the seven doors on Mila's screen. 'Here ... goes ... nothing.'

As soon as he touched the seventh door, the Games Thinker website shimmered and changed.

The DARE winners gaped.

STAY OR SWAP?

As they watched, terrified, a countdown timer appeared and flashed red.

00:59
00:58

'What do we do?' Dylan asked.

Zander jumped off the bench and looked around wildly. 'You want to kill us?' he yelled, beating his chest. 'We are right here! Come on, Rocco, Signmaker, whoever you are— you are a coward!'

Mila wiped tears from her eyes. 'Sorry! We should have left it! Sorry!'

'Which door?' Yasmin asked desperately. 'Which one?'

00:34
00:33

'Quick!' Zander said, circling back. 'Decide!'

'I say we stick with lucky number seven,' Dylan said.

'It hasn't been lucky for us!' Isabel snapped.

'It's a fifty-fifty,' Andy said. 'But we have to choose!'

00:12
00:11

'Seven, it has to be,' Yasmin said. 'Agreed?'

Terrified, the others nodded.

'I'll do it!' Yasmin said, finger reaching for the door on her screen.

'No!' yelled Mila, eyes wild and wide, face frantic with fear. 'I know what this is! It's a trick. *Don't!*'